dear baby girl

Dear Baby Girl

jane*orcutt

tyndale house publishers, inc.
wheaton, illinois

Visit areUthirsty.com

Visit Tyndale's exciting Web site at tyndale.com

thirsty(?) is a trademark of Tyndale House Publishers, Inc.

Designed by Julie Chen

Material for this book was taken from *Lullaby,* ISBN 0-8423-5405-0.

Published in association with the literary agency of Janet Kobobel Grant, Books &
Such, 4788 Carissa Ave., Santa Rosa, CA 95405.

This novel is a work of fiction. Names, characters, places, and incidents either are
the product of the author's imagination or are used fictitiously. Any resemblance
to actual events, locales, organizations, or persons living or dead is entirely
coincidental and beyond the intent of either the author or publisher.

Library of Congress Cataloging-in-Publication Data

Orcutt, Jane.
  Dear baby girl / Jane Orcutt.
    p. cm.
  ISBN 1-4143-0093-X (sc)
  I. Title.
  PS3565.R37D43 2005
813'.54—dc22   2004021388

Printed in the United States of America

08 07 06 05
8 7 6 5 4 3 2 1

to sandra byrd

One

Merrilee Hunter dug into the pockets of her ragged maternity cutoffs and laid the haul on the drugstore's glass counter: a provisional driver's license, one quarter, one dime, two nickels, a piece of string from the hem of the shorts, a half-empty tube of Avon lipstick, and a scrap of paper with a phone number. The paper she hurriedly stuffed back into her pocket, as though the saleswoman on the other side knew exactly what it was.

* * *

1

In a bony ninety-degree angle, the woman leaned over the counter, sifting the money from among Merrilee's possessions, pushing each coin with the pad of her index finger into a pile. "Twenty-five, thirty-five, forty-five." She raised her eyes, then folded her arms against the glass. "You ain't got enough, Merrilee," she said, her voice quivering with triumph. "Popcorn'll cost you forty-nine cents."

Merrilee bit her lip. She slid her open palm across the counter to gather her things, but old man Kenner stepped up beside her and stopped the motion with his gnarled, white-haired hand. Four pennies plunked against the glass. "I'll spot her the rest, Paula Jean. Just go get a bag from the machine before her bus gets here."

Paula Jean bustled toward the other end of the counter, fixing Merrilee with a wrinkled frown as she shoveled the popcorn into a red-and-white striped bag.

Merrilee eased her hand out from under the old man's, ducking her head. "You didn't have to do that, Mr. Kenner," she mumbled. "I can do without."

"Let's just call it one of them bone voyagee gifts, okay, girl?" His gaze dropped to her extended belly, which pressed up hard against the glass counter. He caught her glance and smiled, a leer she recognized

well. "Ain't ever' day a girl like you runs from town,
tail tucked. Now your mama, I coulda seen her doing
something like this, but not you. Thought you had
more spunk."

Merrilee's face warmed, but she didn't respond.

One, two, three . . . Take deep breaths, Merrilee.
Don't let anybody see how you feel.

The baby poked against the counter as if to
break free. Merrilee stepped back.

Mr. Kenner squinted. "You headin' out to look
for that baby's daddy? None of the boys 'round
Palmwood here have 'fessed up, and they generally
brag on accomplishments like you're displayin' so
proudlike."

Merrilee didn't answer. He didn't really want to
know the truth; that was devoured by gossip in this
small town as easily as the Laundromat dryers ate up the
precious quarters Mama used to hoard in her tip jar.

"Here's ya popcorn." Paula Jean shoved the bag
across the counter, her hands stopping well shy of
Merrilee's.

"Thanks." Merrilee lifted the bag, then looked
Paula Jean and Mr. Kenner square in the eye, hoping
for some sort of friendly sign, some expression of farewell. They stared back at her, eyes cold and hard as
the iron gates of Palmwood's cemetery slamming shut.

❋ ❋ ❋

"Well . . ." She gestured toward the door. "Guess I'll wait outside for the bus."

"You do that, hon." Paula Jean wiped down the counter. "Say, Ed, what do you think about the Gophers' chances this fall with their new quarterback? That kid can throw a mighty long pass, I hear."

"Well, now . . ." Mr. Kenner leaned on the counter and launched into a verbal assault on the upcoming team.

Merrilee hefted Mama's battered blue hard-sided suitcase and headed outside. A bell chimed as she exited.

Never send to know for whom the bell tolls; It tolls for thee.

She smiled wryly as she eased down on the wooden bench below the ancient metal Greyhound sign.

Mama would've said the bell was some sort of omen—but good or bad? Her superstitions didn't always make sense and, as far as Merrilee could tell, had no basis in any folklore other than that of her own creation.

"I'm tellin' you, Merrilee," she'd said, pointing with her freshly lit Marlboro for emphasis. "Our lives are ruled by chance. Luck. The best we can do is watch for signs."

"Oh, Mama."

"It's true, girl. Heed the bad ones and grab on to the good ones."

Merrilee decided to humor her. "But how will I know the difference?"

"You'll know." Mama had taken a long drag of the cigarette, blown out the smoke, then ruffled Merrilee's hair. "You'll just know."

It seemed to Merrilee that up until the last seven months, all her knowing had been pretty easy. She'd found, if not all her answers, then most of her peace, at the ramshackle Gospel Fellowship Church building just up the road from the trailer park. When Merrilee was big enough to buckle her own patent leather Sunday shoes, Mama walked with her every week to the church. She'd smile down at Merrilee over an ancient hymnal the Baptists and Methodists had handed down. Merrilee would tuck her hand in Mama's and prop her own hymnal against the back of a splintered pew, gaping at the giant wooden cross down front. Pastor Luke gestured at it every week at the end of the last hymn before he launched into his sermon. "Can you hear him, brothers and sisters?" he might say, after the final verse of "Softly and Tenderly." "Oh, sinner, he's calling you home!"

After a few years, Merrilee grew to understand

why the wooden boards were prominently displayed
up front, and why some church members danced and
clapped their hands with joy during the hymn singing. Mama always just rolled her eyes and smiled
smugly, still believing in luck and good versus bad
signs. One Sunday morning after a long night out
with one of her boyfriends, Mama cracked her bedroom door, a washrag at her forehead, just long
enough to pronounce herself a retired churchgoer.

From then on, eleven-year-old Merrilee walked
the dusty path alone every week to Gospel Fellowship. One Sunday when Pastor Luke gave the altar
call and the choir sang "I Have Decided to Follow
Jesus," she also walked alone down front and
accepted the significance of the wooden cross into her
life. The members of Gospel Fellowship accepted her
as well. They never asked about Mama but welcomed
Merrilee as family. Her new brothers and sisters
walked and talked with her along the spiritual road,
pressing a Bible into her hands, prayers into her ears,
and hope into her heart.

Another kick from the baby, and Merrilee's
smile faded to a frown. She set the striped bag aside,
fluttered a hand over her belly, then reached for the
suitcase. Instead, she settled back, folding her hands
in her lap.

* * *

*Later, on the bus. When it's quieter and I can think
a bit.*

"Merrilee!"

Sylvie Ponds, Palmwood's only librarian, huffed
and waddled her way across the gravel parking lot.
Face flushed with exertion, she fanned her hand
against thin bangs slicked with sweat against her forehead. The sleeves of her polyester polka-dot blouse
strained at her doughy biceps.

Merrilee smiled. "Mornin', Miss Ponds. I told
you there wasn't any need to see me off."

Sylvie heaved herself down on the bench, suck-
ing in gulps of air like a landed catfish. Merrilee
grabbed the popcorn and scooted all the way to the
end of the bench, till one hip hung off. She braced
her feet hard against the ground and held on to the
edge of the seat, between her knees. The baby
kicked, but she ignored it.

"I was . . . afraid I'd miss you, Merrilee." Sylvie
drew one last gulp, then laid a hand over her ample
chest as her normal breath returned. "I couldn't
have you leave without my saying good-bye, now
could I?"

"I'm glad you came." Merrilee glanced at the
drugstore's entrance, then back again. "Truth to tell,
I'm kinda scared. Mama always said someday we'd get

to travel, but I never figured I'd be doing it like this. I feel like I'm sneaking out of town."

Or being run out on a rail.

Sylvie patted her hand. "This is a good Christian place where you're going. They'll take fine care of you. I'll miss you over at the library every week, but the books'll be waiting for you when you get back." She cleared her throat. "And if not those at the Palmwood Library, why, those at another one. Just you keep reading, hear?"

"I will, Miss Ponds," Merrilee said solemnly, though she could no more stop reading than she could stop the birth of this baby. Reading library books took her beyond the dingy trailer she shared with Mama, but reading the Bible took her even farther—beyond herself. Out of all the Gospel Fellowship members, Sylvie Ponds had encouraged Merrilee the most in this direction. In quiet moments at the children's table at the library, they huddled in undersized plastic chairs to study passages of Scripture. Especially the ones about God's love and mercy, which Merrilee clung to, even now.

Sylvie squeezed her hand. "What you're doing—" She blinked hard, then tried again. "What you're doing is about the most selfless thing I ever knew anybody to do."

* * *

Embarrassed, Merrilee looked away.

A large silver bus pulled into the parking lot, splaying gravel, its destination shining plainly above the driver's head: Austin. Merrilee thought it might as well have said Exit.

She rose, gripping the worn handle of the suitcase in one hand and the popcorn bag in another. "I guess this is it," she said, trying to smile.

Sylvie rose too, shading her eyes against the sun. "You have a safe trip, okay?" She paused, lowering her voice. "You're a good girl, Merrilee. Don't let anybody tell you different."

Merrilee nodded, but her heart sank clear to the bulge in her belly. She tried to speak, but the words caught in her throat. Where would she have been the last few years without Sylvie Ponds? She couldn't have made this difficult decision without Sylvie's guidance and love, especially now that Mama was gone and nearly everyone else had turned away.

The doors to the bus hissed open, and the weary-looking driver trudged down the stairs. He held out his hand for Merrilee's bag in a gesture of bored impatience.

Sylvie patted Merrilee's shoulder, then pulled her into a quick hug. They'd never touched before, and Merrilee felt the awkwardness between them as

* * *

wide as the baby that separated them from a full embrace.

Sylvie stepped back quickly as if she felt it too, then smiled lopsidedly. "Go on with you, then. Go see what they got to offer in Austin. Try to make it to the capitol if you can."

Merrilee nodded.

"And drop me a postcard!"

The driver stepped forward. "Miss? Your bag?"

Merrilee clutched the handle tighter. "I'll just carry it with me, thanks."

He shrugged and headed for the bus. "All right, but we need to get going."

Merrilee followed, then turned. "Bye, Miss Ponds. Thank you for . . ."

Sylvie smiled. "It's okay, Merrilee." Her voice softened. "It'll be okay. I'll be praying for you. 'Where two or more are gathered,' remember?"

Merrilee glanced over her shoulder and saw Paula Jean and Mr. Kenner standing in the drugstore doorway. Neither waved. Neither smiled. *There goes Faye Hunter's daughter*, their faces said.

Merrilee turned away and boarded the bus. She bumped and jostled her way down the narrow aisle, past four other souls who stared listlessly out windows with no latches. She took the seat farthest back, next to the bathroom, then cradled the suitcase and pop-corn bag against herself. She closed her eyes and didn't open them even when the bus shifted from gravel to pavement and lumbered down the two-lane road.

When she knew they must be well out of town, she propped the popcorn bag against the armrest of the adjoining empty seat and balanced the suitcase on her knees. She popped open the rusty clasps, then pulled out a ragged pastel cloth journal and a pen. Making a desk of the closed suitcase, she opened the book to the next white page, blank and crisp.

Nipping the cap off with her teeth, she poised the pen over the paper for a moment, then wrote slowly and carefully, the way Miss Percy had taught her all the way back in second grade.

> *Dear Baby Girl,*
>
> *In all my fifteen years of growing up, I never once thought about what it'd be like for a new mama to leave the hospital with her baby in another pair of arms. I guess I've always fancied the notion of a perfect family, with the daddy beaming over his wife and new child, maybe even a grandma or two hovering nearby, knitting booties or something.*

*I don't know why I think like that, since
I never even knew my own daddy. All Mama
ever said was that he'd loved her but not
enough to stick around. Except for times like
father-daughter banquets, I never really missed
having a daddy, though. I had Mama. Or at
least I always thought I'd have her.*

*I've prayed about what I'm doing a lot,
and this seems to be God's answer. Pastor Luke
thought so when I talked to him about it. So
did Sylvie Ponds. They're the only two folks in
town who don't look sideways at me for carrying
you. Even Mama had her druthers about
your life . . . .*

Merrilee paused long enough to scoop a left-
handed fistful of popcorn into her mouth. She started
to write more, but the achy place inside her heart
simmered like water on a back burner. She carefully
placed the pen in the journal's gutter and set the suitcase and book in the next seat, then wiped her greasy
hand on her shorts.

Tucking her legs up under herself awkwardly,
she curled up into the seat and stared out the window. Her face reflected back in the fingerprint-

smudged glass, and she glanced away. Anyway, the prairie grass and scrub cedars looked the same as they did around Palmwood and probably wouldn't give way to anything prettier before the bus got to Austin.

Mama had been to Austin several times, she'd told Merrilee. Once when she was in a high school track meet—she'd been pretty good back in her day at jumping the hurdles and running sprints, she'd bragged. Then later with some man for a weekend, just for a lark.

Mighta been my daddy, for all I know. Maybe that's where they brought me into being. Wouldn't that be funny, me bringing this baby back to be born where I came from?

Merrilee popped open the suitcase again and slipped her hand inside the frayed elastic side pouch, fingers digging for the carefully trimmed photo she'd downloaded at the library. The paper was already worn around the edges from too much handling, even though she'd never shown it to anyone, not even Miss Ponds.

She squinted at the photo, trying to pretend she'd never seen it before. As if she'd just turned the page of a picture album and come across this couple with their dog—which is exactly how she'd found them on the Internet through the Palmwood public library's lone computer. It'd taken her days to work

* * *

up the courage to even access the Austin adoption agency's Web page, but once she had, she'd listlessly paged through image after identical image of smiling, hopeful couples.

Merrilee fingered the scrap of paper in her pocket. They had no idea she was even on her way. The agency said she could call them when she got to town, if she wanted to wait. It was her decision, they said. All the arrangements were hers to decide.

Merrilee shivered. She squeezed her eyes shut and wrapped her arms around her thick waist, swaying slightly to a gentle hum. "'Jesus loves me, this I know. For the Bible tells me so. . . .'"

The bus rumbled closer to Austin, and bit by bit, Merrilee finished the popcorn. The saltiness made her throat burn, but she doggedly finished it all. Mr. Kenner didn't pay those four cents for her to waste.

In proportion to the bag emptying, however, her fears multiplied. What if no one was there to meet her? She didn't even have enough money to use a pay phone. Would someone loan her a quarter? Or what if Adoption Lifeline had changed its mind about accepting her? Maybe they didn't have enough room, or maybe they didn't want someone as young as her, from a small hick town.

She squeezed her eyes shut against the rising

* * *

panic. *God, oh, God. I have nowhere to go now. I have nowhere to go later.*

"This is Austin," the driver announced loudly, so that Merrilee could hear. He looked in the rear-view mirror, even though she knew he couldn't see her sitting all the way at the back. "This is where you get off."

Merrilee crumpled the empty bag and tucked it into her shorts pocket. It felt greasy, but she couldn't just leave it on the seat for someone else to clean up. She'd already stashed her belongings back in the suitcase, which she gripped by the handle and balanced beside her on the floor. The bus lurched into the station, halted, and she was there.

The station bustled with activity—furloughed soldiers playing cards while they waited for buses to take them home, elderly women disembarking into loved one's arms, businessmen in polyester suits buying tickets at the counter. Merrilee clung to the suitcase, her fears rising on a wave of too much popcorn and too little hope. She lowered her gaze, concentrating on the dirty linoleum.

"Merrilee?"

She raised her gaze hesitantly. "Yeah?"

An older woman with bobbed gray hair smiled. "I'm Martha Pennywood, the matron at Adoption

Lifeline's residence facility." She held out her hand. "It's nice to meet you."

"Uh, nice to meet you too." She shifted the suitcase to her left hand and shook Mrs. Penny-wood's.

The woman tsk-tsked and took the suitcase from her. "Let me carry that for you. You must be tired from your trip and anxious to get settled. It's just a short walk to my car, then a short drive and we'll be home."

Merrilee breathed a sigh of relief. *Home.* It might be temporary, but it was somewhere . . . for now.

****

Nora Rey fled from the Mother's Day service at church. As usual, the priest had honored the mothers among the congregation, and she had felt singled out—again—for what felt more and more, year after year, like failure. Her husband, Steven, as usual, seemed to understand.

Safely inside the Lexus, neither spoke as they headed toward the hills west of Austin and the security of home. Nora studied Steven's hand as it controlled the gearshift with masculine firmness.

It was his hands that had attracted her to him,

hands so smooth yet confident as they dissected speci-
mens in their biology lab at the University of Texas
long ago. Hands that would later perform delicate
orthopedic surgery. Hands that would join with hers
on their wedding day, and for twenty-three years
since, but that could never do enough to fill the
emptiness of her arms.

The years had passed, one after another, in a
succession of torn calendar pages and monthly tears
of failure. Specialists were consulted and options
weighed, but even medicine couldn't undo what
had apparently been ordained. Steven tentatively
broached the subject of adoption. Nora gratefully
agreed, relieved to abandon the heart-wrenching pain
of each month's failure. Surely *now* God would grant
her a child.

Yet three years of waiting had passed—marked
by daily, rather than monthly, failure—as younger
couples were repeatedly selected by birth mothers to
be the parents of their children. Apparently Nora's
adoptive clock was winding down as rapidly as her
biological one had.

Steven pulled off Ranch Road 2222 and onto
the gravel road that wound its way to their lakefront
property. He mashed the remote-control button, and
the privacy gate swung open. They drove up the road

* * *

toward the dream home that felt to Nora more every day like a yellow brick shell.

Inside the garage Steven parked the car beside Nora's SUV. She reached the house first, listlessly tossing her purse on the kitchen counter. Beyond, Lake Travis sparkled through the expansive living room's floor-to-ceiling windows.

She felt Steven's hands on her shoulders. "Want to go for a swim? Or a boat ride?"

Nora shook her head. Patient Steven always understood.

"Please, Nora?"

She turned. His forty-sixth birthday was in three months, and while he was still handsome and youthful from tennis, waterskiing, and swimming, he had developed age lines around his eyes. Nora laid her hand against his cheek and smiled. How could she refuse him anything? "A swim in the pool might be nice."

Steven smiled, and the lines deepened. "Put your suit on, Blondie," he said, popping her affectionately on the backside. "I'll meet you outside." Whistling, he loosened his tie and headed toward the back door that led down the steps to the pool.

Nora grinned, knowing that he'd probably worn his swim trunks under his suit in anticipation of an afternoon outdoors. She wondered what his patients—especially the more conservative, elderly ones—would think if they knew how unconventional Dr. Rey really was.

In the spacious, orderly walk-in closet, Nora changed out of her suit and carefully hung it next to the others. She pulled on her favorite swimsuit, the size six white one-piece that best complemented her tan, then scooped up a beach towel. Pulling back her hair with a terry-cloth band, she followed Steven's trail of shoes, socks, suit coat, pants, and tie as she passed through the kitchen and hallway. Fingering the collar from the shirt hanging on the back-door knob, she smiled.

Outside, Lucky bounded toward her and barked an enthusiastic greeting. The German shepherd wound around Nora, bumping against her hips. He nuzzled his head against her hand. Laughing, she rubbed his ears affectionately. "Poor old Lucky. You think you're a cat, don't you?"

At the sound of her voice, he sat back on his haunches and stared at her imploringly.

"Lucky!" Steven called. Quickly transferring his affection, the dog loped down the grassy slope toward the swimming pool. Steven threw a tattered tennis shoe across the slope, and Lucky gave chase.

* * *

"Thanks." Nora descended the stairs to the pool area. "Sometimes his affection can be—"

"Annoying?"

"Embarrassing."

Nora draped her towel over the back of a chaise lounge, then slathered her arms with sunblock. She leaned over to apply lotion to her legs, and when she straightened, Steven was treading water in the deep end, watching her.

She moved to the edge of the water's deep end and studied the bouncing reflection of the sun and the ripples of light at the bottom of the pool. Up from the lake behind her roared the sound of a boat, punctuated by squeals of children being towed on an inner tube.

Closing her eyes, Nora hooked her toes around the rough concrete edge, bent her knees, and leaned forward. She broke the surface cleanly in one fluid movement. Underwater, life hung suspended, muted. She pushed back to the surface in long, clean strokes, and when she broke free, Steven was waiting beside her.

"Nice dive," he said.

Nora started swimming away. "Thanks. Race you to the shallow end."

"Hey! No head starts!" Steven splashed after her, and they reached the pool steps at the same time.

* * *

Breathless, they fell across each other in a wet tangle, laughing.

Nora leaned back against Steven, resting her head against his shoulder. He loosened the hair band with his fingers, fanning her hair against the water. She closed her eyes, feeling her stomach tighten as his fingers trailed the strap of her swimsuit.

"Nora," he said softly, "about the church service today . . . maybe next year we shouldn't go."

Next year. "Shh." She'd nearly forgotten, in the sweetness of being at home. She had so many blessings—was it selfish to want more? And yet motherhood, so basic, so biological, didn't seem to be part of God's plan for her life. His purpose was larger than her desires, yet not having even a glimpse of his blueprints was often so difficult.

Show me. Please show me.

"I love you," Steven whispered into the curve of her neck. "We're in this together."

She squeezed her eyes shut, the ache rising to her throat.

Steven's cell phone rang sharply, slicing the moment. He exhaled with resignation and released her. "It's probably about Mrs. Wimbers and her hip replacement. When I saw her on rounds yesterday, she was having a lot of pain."

* * *

He grabbed the phone and a towel at the same time, already rubbing his hair. "Steven Rey."

The water lapped against Nora's too-flat stomach, and she extended her arms for balance. She turned her head against the glare of sunlight across the pool's surface, winking back tears.

"No, we didn't know." Steven bent to scribble on a pad of paper. "We'll check it out. . . . Yes . . . We'll contact you as soon as possible." He set the phone back on the table, then stared out at the lake.

Nora sighed. The day felt broken, ruined. "Trouble?"

Steven turned, a goofy grin on his face, like the day the dentist had given him laughing gas to remove an impacted wisdom tooth. "We've been chosen," he said.

She stared blankly. "Chosen for what?"

"Chosen as adoptive parents. A birth mother saw us on Adoption Lifeline's Web site and moved into the agency just yesterday. They called to say she'd left us an e-mail. Nora! She wants to talk to us about raising her baby."

Nora drew a deep breath, tightening her arms to maintain her balance. Her heart beat quickly, singing against her ribs.

Steven walked to the pool steps and held out his

hands to help her stand. "Before we call . . . ," he said, squeezing her hands.

"Yes," Nora murmured in agreement, bowing her head as Steven prayed aloud for the young girl and her baby, for their own desire to raise a child. For the first time in a long while, hope filled the voice of his petition.

Steven logged on to the Internet, his hands still damp. Standing behind him, Nora curled her fingers around his towel-wrapped shoulders, holding her breath as she leaned over to watch the mail screen pop up.

"We have eleven messages," Steven announced unnecessarily, scrolling through the list.

Nora dragged an antique Windsor chair beside Steven's ergonomic one. "I wonder why she didn't phone."

Steven shrugged, his eyes trained on the screen. "The agency said we can call her. Here's the e-mail, the last one. It's from . . . Fatgirl."

"Fatgirl?" Nora had always pictured their birth mother as a slim, beautiful cheerleader who'd gotten caught up in the throes of passion with an athletic boyfriend.

Steven poised the cursor over the on-screen envelope. "Ready?"

* * *

Nora nodded. Steven double-clicked the mouse, and they both leaned forward.

> *Dear Nora and Steven,*
> *I saw your picture on the Adoption Lifeline Web page. You look very nice. I like your house and your dog too. Please call me at the agency if you want to talk. My name is Merrilee Hunter.*

"Merrilee," Nora whispered. It was a pretty, old-fashioned sort of name. At least it worked to dispel the image "Fatgirl" invoked. Given the two discordant pieces of information, Nora pictured a stocky girl with a ponytail, dressed in a gingham shirt and jeans.

"She didn't give us much to go on." Steven pushed back his chair. "Do you want to call, or should I?"

"We can each get on an extension." Nora rose, shivering as air blasted from the vent and chilled her wet swimsuit. "Don't you think we should change clothes first?"

"She might decide we're not interested and leave for a while," Steven said, the practical surgeon taking over.

* * *

24

Nora nodded. "I'll go to the kitchen phone.
Will you do the talking, to start us off?" Working as a
real estate agent had wrung any shyness from her per-
sonality, but now her hands shook as she lifted the
phone from the marble countertop. Steven was more
accustomed to taking charge in delicate situations.

"They're calling her to the phone!"

Nora pressed the receiver's Talk button just as
the phone was picked up at the other end.

"Hello?"

Nora gripped the countertop, her heart pounding. *Say something, Steven. And please let it be good.*

"Merrilee? This is Dr. Rey."

There was a pause at the other end. "Dr. who?"

"Rey. Steven Rey. My wife and I posted on the
Adoption Lifeline Web page. . . . Are you Merrilee?"

"Oh, Steven. Of course! I forgot you were a
doctor. You're a doctor of . . . of . . ."

"Orthopedics," he said, then added, "A bone
doctor."

"Oh! I see," Merrilee said, though she sounded
like she didn't.

Steven cleared his throat. "Merrilee, my wife,
Nora, is on the line too."

"Hello, Merrilee," Nora said in the calmest
voice she could muster. What had the adoption

agency suggested as an opening line with a birth mother? "How are you feeling?"

"Pretty good. It's kinda hard to sleep at night, what with my belly being so big. But other'n that, I can't complain."

Nora swallowed hard. "How far along are you?"

"Near as I can guess, I'd say seven months."

"You haven't been to a doctor?" Steven said.

Nora held her breath, hoping he hadn't offended the girl.

"Not yet. I haven't had the money. But the agency said they . . . well, I guess you . . . would pay for things like that. If we decide to make the swap, that is."

The swap? Nora frowned, walking back to the office where Steven sat. He saw the expression on her face and put a finger to his lips. "The agency said you just came to Austin yesterday, Merrilee," he said. "Where's your hometown?"

"Nearby. Palmwood."

Nora and Steven exchanged glances. Palmwood was scarcely a blip on the highway from Austin to Houston. "Do you like it here so far? Austin, I mean. And at Adoption Lifeline?" he said.

"I guess so. I'm still settling in. My room's real pretty."

A muffled popping sound indicated Merrilee
was probably wrapping the telephone cord around
her fingers. Nora also heard a rhythmic *squeak-creak*
and realized the girl was sitting in a rocking chair.

"Merrilee," she said softly, "what made you
contact us today?" She paused. "Did you know it's
Mother's Day?"

The chair's tempo increased. "Yes, ma'am, I do.
I been thinking about my own mama most of the
day. That's why I needed to come to Austin."

"But did you want to come?" Steven said.

There was a pause at the other end of the line.
"Yeah."

Nora drew a deep, happy breath. She and Steven
smiled at each other over their respective receivers.
"Name the day, and we'd be delighted to meet you,"
he said.

"I guess Wednesday would do fine. Mrs. Pennywood wants me to see a doctor."

"Wednesday it is." Steven doodled the word on
a pad of paper. "What would you like to do?"

"The agency said sometimes people like to
eat supper together or something." She hesitated.
"It don't . . . er, doesn't have to be anything fancy.
I don't want to impose."

Impose? "We'd be delighted to have dinner with

* * *
27

you," Nora said. "We know many wonderful restaurants, and it would be our pleasure to treat you and get to know you. And let you get to know us too."

"Okay."

Nora gave Steven a thumbs-up but was surprised to see him frowning, like he did whenever a patient wasn't being totally honest with him. The girl's tone was definitely more subdued than when the conversation began—did he think she was entertaining second thoughts? Nora started to ask, but Steven put a finger to his lips.

"There are so many adoptive families listed on the agency's Web page," he said gently. "Why did you choose us to call?"

They heard her draw a soft breath. "Because your dog's name is Lucky."

Two

Merrilee sat cross-legged on her bed and eyed the starchy white curtains of her window. She was still afraid someone would haul her away from the adoption agency's residential home, declaring that she didn't belong.

She didn't. This room with its clean curtains and shining clear window, gleaming hardwood floors, and matching white wicker furniture was foreign to anything she'd ever had at the trailer. She'd been here

* * *

29

three days now and still hadn't unpacked, despite the
residential mother's warm assurance that this was,
indeed, her home for the next two months.

She rose slowly, fighting the ungainly balance
of her body. Smoothing her hair, she peered into the
wicker-framed mirror. One of the other girls had
loaned her a pair of navy blue maternity pants and
a bright flowered shirt to wear for her first meeting
with the family that would adopt her baby. Mrs.
Pennywood said it was normal to feel nervous and
that she should relax and enjoy getting to know the
couple. And most importantly, dear, she should listen
to her heart as to whether these were the people she
wanted to raise her child.

Merrilee dug into her suitcase, hesitated, then lifted
a Polaroid snapshot of Mama. It was the only photo she
had of her mother by herself—one of the few photos
she had of her mother, period. The three others either
had a then-current boyfriend or Merrilee in the picture.
Merrilee trimmed the images of the boyfriends, but
Mama always looked lopsided somehow.

In this picture, Mama was holding a beer can in
one hand and a cigarette in the other. She was smiling, and Merrilee knew it wasn't one of her fake
photo smiles because she herself had taken the picture
last summer.

* * *

Lucas Procter shoved the camera into her hands when the three of them were barbecuing outside the trailer. "Get a good picture of your mama now, Merrilee," Lucas said. "Ain't she a dish? This'll give you something to remember her by when you're a mama yourself."

"That won't be for a long, long time, Lucas," Mama said, laughing. She leaned up against the redwood picnic table one of her past boyfriends had stolen from a roadside park. Posing for the camera, Mama smiled at Merrilee. "You're not going to get tangled up with boys for a long time, are you, sugar? Have yourself some fun just being a girl for a while, right?"

Merrilee sighted Mama in the viewfinder and grinned. "Right, Mama." It was their secret conversation, their inside joke kept from Mama's boyfriends. She liked each one of them well enough, but Merrilee had seen over the years, even if Mama hadn't said a word, that men weren't always the most reliable creatures God ever made.

Mama smiled back, holding up the beer can like a trophy and the cigarette between two fingers of the other hand. She tilted her head back and pouted like a 1930s movie star. She winked *at Merrilee, who was too mesmerized to take the photo. Mama probably wasn't what most people would call beautiful, but she managed to snag attention—especially from men—wherever she went. In her presence, Merrilee often felt like not only a shadow of Faye Hunter, but of herself as well.*

"Snap the picture, Merrilee," Mama had said through her posed expression, and the moment was segmented from time, frozen.

Merrilee wedged the photo into the bottom corner of the mirror's wicker frame, then touched the image of Mama's face. Beside that photo she placed the one of Mama and her together, the one Boone Samson had taken of them at Merrilee's fourth birthday party at McDonald's. It'd been just the three of them at the fast-food place—no streamers, cake, or other kids to celebrate—but it'd been a good party all the same. Merrilee had liked Boone, probably better than any of Mama's other boyfriends, before or since. At age four, she'd foolishly thought that they'd be a real family, but he'd eventually left Mama and Merrilee by themselves, like all the rest.

Merrilee touched the worn leather Bible that had once been Mama's. Merrilee had set it out beneath the mirror when she first arrived here, but she'd been too ashamed to read it alone for a long while now.

A knock sounded at the door before it swung open. Sheryl Billups stuck her head into the room, then the rest of her nineteen-year-old pregnant body followed. "Hey, girl. Whatcha doing?"

Merrilee stepped away from the mirror. "Just getting settled."

"You've been doing that for three days now," Sheryl said, levering herself onto the bed and hugging a decorative pillow. "Don't you like it here?"

"It's all right."

"All right?" Sheryl sat up, grinning. "Just wait till you meet the parents. They treat you like a queen around here, but these parents are so eager to have a baby, they'll do just about anything you want." She lowered her voice. "Why do you think I'm having a second baby? I learned the first time that a girl can make a little extra money, get a few little trinkets for herself."

Merrilee frowned. "We're not supposed to take gifts. Or money."

Sheryl shrugged. "Who has to know? Besides, the parents are so grateful to you, what does it hurt? It makes them feel good, and you might as well make a little something for yourself for all you're going through."

Merrilee rubbed her belly thoughtfully.

"That's right." Sheryl grinned, watching Merrilee's hand. "You're growing a gold mine there. Take what you can. You've been left high and dry, haven't you? Isn't it nice to live in this place where nobody yells at you and no man comes sniffing around? Yeah, we have to go to a weekly Bible study, since this is a Christian joint, but you seen that swimming pool outside? the meals they serve here? You get anything like that at your home? I sure didn't."

She leaned back. "I may just do this every couple of years. If nothing else it gets me away from Gary for a few months."

"Is that your boyfriend?"

"No, my husband. But he doesn't want kids, so this is the second I'm giving up. I had an abortion four years ago, but trust me, this is the life. Nobody cared about me then. Why, I had to drive myself home from the clinic. My parents called me trash, and my boyfriend never spoke to me again. But let the world know you're planning to put a baby up for adoption and they think you're a saint."

"That's not what it was like for me," Merrilee whispered. "Everybody in Palmwood looked at me

hateful-like, the bigger I got. It would have been easier to have an abortion, but Mama—" She bit her lip,
glancing at the photos on the mirror.

Sheryl eased up from the bed and headed for the
door. "Just wait till you meet the couple you chose—
that's today, isn't it? They'll treat you so fine, you'll
forget all about your hometown. And you just sit
back and let them pamper you, okay? You've
deserved it." She shut the door behind her.

Merrilee sat on the bed, deflated, her enthusiasm
dampened for meeting the Reys. She squeezed her
eyes shut, so she wouldn't be tempted to glance at
Mama's pictures again, and prayed hard.

When Mrs. Pennywood knocked, Merrilee was
still sitting on the bed. "They've arrived, dear," the
elderly woman said from the doorway. "They look
as nice as their picture."

Merrilee rose, fighting the fear that churned in
her belly, all around her baby. "I . . . I'm ready."

"You look very nice." Mrs. Pennywood smiled,
smoothing Merrilee's hair.

As she lumbered down the stairs behind the
residential mother, Merrilee didn't feel nice. Maybe
they'd think she was too fat. Maybe they wouldn't
like her clothes. Maybe they wouldn't like the way
she talked.

* * *

Maybe they'd decide they didn't want her baby.
She didn't think she could go through all those
photos of hopeful couples again.

Mrs. Pennywood led her into the closed-off
room with the velveteen furniture that Merrilee was
afraid to sit on. Mrs. Pennywood used it primarily for
important meetings, and its formality reminded
Merrilee of a nineteenth-century parlor.

"Here she is," Mrs. Pennywood said, her voice
bright as she opened the door.

A man with medium-brown hair and a trim figure, dressed in tan pants and a colorful sports shirt,
straightened from where he leaned against the sofa.

A woman sat on the sofa, leafing through a mag-
azine, her face tense, her mouth set in a tight expression. She looked perfect—blonde hair swept up and
back into a stylish ponytail, gold earrings, and a fash-
ionable pink pantsuit. She looked like a cover model,
and when she smiled at Merrilee, her lipstick looked
perfect, her teeth like a TV ad for toothpaste.

Merrilee smiled, but it felt fake, her teeth probably
showing as large as a horse's. Mrs. Pennywood stepped
back, leaving her open and vulnerable. "Hi," she said,
and her voice came out as a squeak. She clasped her
hands in front of her belly. "I'm Merrilee."

The man moved toward her with a hand

* * *

extended. "Hi, Merrilee. I'm Dr. Rey . . . Steven."
When he shook her hand, his felt firm and warm.

"Merrilee." The woman rose, nodding, then
extended her hand. It felt cool and slim, like the rest
of her looked. "I'm Nora Rey. We're so glad to meet
you."

"Me too," she said, then couldn't think of anything else. She dipped her head, letting her bangs fall
into her eyes.

She felt Mrs. Pennywood's hand at her shoulder.
"I usually find that the introduction's the most difficult
part of the first meeting. You've all passed with flying
colors." She laughed lightly, and Steven and Nora
joined in. Merrilee smiled and felt her stomach lurch.

"So often a neutral location goes a long way to
ease the awkwardness," Mrs. Pennywood said. "Why
don't you three go get acquainted? Merrilee, feel free
to knock on my door when you get back if you want
to talk."

"Yes, ma'am. Thank you." She smiled, feeling
a rush of relief. If only talking to the Reys was as easy
as talking to Mrs. Pennywood.

"Shall we go?" Steven held the door open, and
Merrilee, feeling embarrassed, scurried through. She
sensed Nora following behind her at a more mature
pace.

* * *

Steven headed toward a Lexus, and Merrilee's eyes widened. "Wow! This is your car?"

Steven clicked the security button on his key chain, smiling. "Would you like to ride in the front seat?"

"Sure!" She turned toward Nora, her expression falling. "If it's all right with you, Mrs. Rey."

"Nora," she said, nodding that regal head. "And no, I don't mind."

Inside the car Steven inserted the key in the ignition. "Where would you like to eat?"

Amazed by the car's interior, Merrilee forgot her nervousness. "Wow! Look at this radio! This CD player! And tinted windows, even!" Mama's old pickup hadn't even had air-conditioning, and the AM-only radio had busted long ago.

From the backseat, Nora leaned between Steven and Merrilee. "Where would you like to eat, dear?" she said.

Jolted back to reality, Merrilee panicked. She tried to think of restaurants she'd seen from the bus window when she pulled into town. "Uh, Chili's would be nice." She fumbled for the seat belt and clumsily buckled it over her stomach.

Nora's smile looked patient, like one of Merrilee's teachers when she couldn't come up with the right answer. "Wouldn't you rather go to a . . .

quieter place? Steven and I frequent a restaurant that has peacocks on the grounds and—"

"Peacocks squawk a lot," Merrilee said without thinking, then covered her mouth with her hand. "I . . . I'm sorry. That was rude. I don't mind going there."

"Chili's is fine." Steven started the car, and Nora sat back. Merrilee faced forward, clutching her hands in her lap, unsettled.

All the way to the restaurant, she told herself it wasn't going to work. She was just too different from these people. The agency had stressed that in what they called an open adoption, everyone should get along. After all, they would be sharing the child's lifetime, should Merrilee choose to stay involved. She couldn't, but that didn't change matters.

Settled into a Chili's booth across from the Reys, Merrilee covertly eyed Nora while the woman studied the menu. Merrilee thought she had a pretty face, even prettier than Mama's, then chided herself for being disloyal. She yanked the menu up to cover her own face.

The waiter stood at the edge of the table.

"What would you like, Merrilee?" Steven said.

Panic set in again. She hadn't read a word of the menu, but she didn't want to look like someone who couldn't make up her own mind. "Uh, I'd like a Sprite and a hamburger with that hickory sauce. And some onion rings . . ." Maybe she was being too free with the Reys' money. She glanced up at Steven. "If that's okay."

"Sure." Steven turned to the waiter. "Did you get her order?"

"Uh-huh. For you, ma'am?"

Nora firmly shut her menu. "A glass of iced tea and a grilled-chicken Caesar salad. And please go light on the dressing."

"Yes, ma'am. For you, sir?"

"I think a hamburger sounds good too." Steven winked at Merrilee. "And an order of French fries and a Dr Pepper."

Merrilee wanted to sink into the booth. Nora had ordered a salad. She probably thought Merrilee wasn't eating healthy enough for the baby.

To her surprise, Nora smiled, leaning forward on her crossed arms. "What would you like us to know about you, Merrilee?"

Surprised by the woman's abruptness, Merrilee sat up straighter. "What do you want to know?"

"Well, I suppose for starters, how old are you?"

"Fifteen." Right now, despite the baby in her belly, she felt like only five.

"Does the father of your baby know you're here?" Steven said. "Has he signed any papers?"

They were really jumping in with the tough questions. "No, sir." Merrilee swallowed hard. "He never knew about this baby. By the time I found out I was pregnant, he'd left town. We finally heard he'd been killed in a bar up in Oklahoma. Got cut up pretty good, from what they said."

"I'm sorry," Steven said. "You must have been devastated."

Merrilee shrugged. "I'm sorry he's dead, but Wayne and I weren't that close."

Nora's eyebrows drew together, and Merrilee hastily changed the subject. "What else do you want to know? I'm about seven months pregnant . . . I think. This baby sure kicks a lot, and I'm carrying it high. Mama used to say those were two signs you were carrying a girl. I hope so because I'd really like it to be a little girl." She paused, fearful that she'd said the wrong thing. "Do you want a boy?"

Nora and Steven looked at each other. "We've never discussed it," Steven said. "We told the agency that we'd accept either gender."

"Oh. Well, I know men generally seem to want a boy."

"It doesn't matter either way," Nora said. "We would welcome and love a boy or a girl. The doctor may want to do a sonogram . . . sort of an X-ray to

* * *

check on the baby," she added, as if she didn't think
Merrilee would understand. "They can often tell
whether it's a boy or a girl. Would you like to know
in advance, or would you prefer to wait until the
baby's born?"

Merrilee paused, considering. She hadn't realized
she'd be given a choice. "I wouldn't mind knowing,"
she said. "That way, you could name it in advance.
Talk to it and stuff."

"What would you name a girl?" Steven said.
"Have you thought about it?"

She shook her head. She and Mama had never
gotten around to talking about it.

"What about a boy?"

Merrilee hunched her shoulders. It was nice of
them to pretend they cared about her opinion, but it
would be their baby. Not hers.

"Would you want to name him after his father?"
Nora asked.

Did they have to bring up Wayne again? "No,"
she said flatly, then added, to stop any further talk,
"I don't guess it's my place to be naming the kid,
anyway. You two would do that." She paused. "I bet
you could pick a good name for the baby. I like that
you named your dog Lucky."

"You mentioned on the phone that you picked

Nora and me because of that. Why is the name so appealing to you?"

Merrilee felt a sudden urge to laugh. Maybe they were afraid she'd want them to name the baby after the dog. They looked so serious, so intent on getting to the bottom of something that seemed so major to them. She supposed they had a right to worry about who she was, what her thoughts were, where she came from. She would have to tell them just enough not to make them nervous. "Why did you give him that name?" she countered.

Steven glanced at Nora. "A neighbor of ours, a vet, found a puppy by the side of the road between our properties. Probably somebody abandoned him, then tried to run over him. Both his hips were broken. We rushed the dog in and immediately operated. We saved his life, but my neighbor already owned several dogs, so Nora and I agreed to keep him. He's been with us five years now."

"Do you like dogs, Merrilee?" Nora said.

"Not really. Especially if they're big."

Nora glanced at Steven, then at Merrilee. "Lucky's a pretty big dog. He's a German shepherd. But he's as docile as a lamb."

"Oh, I'm not worried about the baby's safety or anything like that. I know you'd take good care of her."

Steven's eyebrows knit together, and Merrilee could imagine him as a doctor puzzling over a medical problem. "But you didn't tell us why our dog's name means so much to you," he said gently.

She struggled for the right words. Most folks didn't understand Mama's thinking or even try to see things from where she sat. "My mother used to say that our lives are ruled by chance and that I should watch for signs to know what to do. The good signs, that is," she added hastily, in case they thought she had a tendency to lean toward evil. "Mama believed those signs were sent by God to guide us. She said that sometimes when she couldn't hear his voice— probably because her ears were too stopped up—he'd talk to her in other ways."

"And you think Lucky's name is some sort of sign?" Nora said.

Merrilee glanced down at the paper place mat, focusing on the cartoonish chili pepper to keep her composure. She didn't want to cry. She wouldn't cry. "It just hit me that if you thought your dog was lucky, how much more would my baby be, if you were to raise her. She needs a good home with good parents."

"What do your parents think about your pregnancy?" Steven said.

"I don't have a daddy, and Mama . . ." Merrilee drew a deep breath and focused on the pepper until it blurred. "Mama died just about a month ago."

She felt a cool hand on her arm, and when she glanced up, she was surprised to see tears in Nora's eyes. "I'm so sorry, Merrilee," she whispered. "You're a brave girl."

Merrilee smiled. "That's what Miss Ponds says. She's Palmwood's librarian and just about my only friend."

Nora glanced at Steven. "Do you spend a lot of time at the library?" he said.

"Oh yes! I work there part-time, but even when I'm not working, I'm usually down there looking at magazines and books. Or the Internet. That's how I found Adoption Lifeline when I decided this baby needed a home."

"When did you decide that?" Nora said softly.

Merrilee glanced down at the place mat again. "Right after Mama's funeral." She drew a deep breath, then looked up. "If you don't mind, I need to ask some questions of my own now. I read this book called *Adoption Guide for the Average Joe and Jill*, and it said the birth mother should ask certain questions too. I've got 'em memorized."

Steven smiled at Nora. They clasped hands

* * *

above the table, and Nora suppressed what sounded suspiciously to Merrilee like a giggle, only she wouldn't think a woman like Nora Rey ever giggled in her life.

"What?" Merrilee said, feeling heat rise to her face. "Don't you think I should ask a few things about you two as well? I'm not giving this baby to just anybody."

"Of course not," Steven said, sobering, glancing at Nora.

Nora took Merrilee's hand. "I'm sorry. We didn't mean to offend you. It's just that we read the same book too and made a mental note on the way over here of what we should ask."

Merrilee smiled. "You must like books."

"We like to read," Nora said. "And yes, we have an extensive collection of books at our house. They feel like old friends."

Merrilee felt a rightness settle in her stomach. "So you'd read to the baby? That's really important to me. I want her to love reading as much as I do."

"We'd read every night before prayers and bed," Nora said. "And during the day too. I'd start with simple picture books, and as she grew older, we'd move up to Dr. Seuss and Little Golden Books, then chapter books. I'd do everything I could to ensure

* * *

that she loved reading, but I would never force her to read. It should be a pleasure, not a punishment."

Merrilee let out a deep breath. "I'm glad to hear it. I hated when teachers would do that to kids who didn't like to read. Seems like it just made them hate reading more."

The server brought their food, halting the conversation. Merrilee dug in, carefully chewing and swallowing the hickory-sauced hamburger with pleasure. She hadn't eaten one since the last time she'd visited Mama at work at the café. Over the years, Mr. Gleason, the owner, had always welcomed Merrilee, even occasionally given her lunch on the house.

But that last time, Mr. Gleason stayed back in his office, as far from both of them as possible. By then, most of the town behaved likewise, what with Merrilee starting to stick out so obvious-like. She wasn't the first unwed teenage girl in town, but she was the only one who didn't have a boy step forward and claim responsibility. The town treated her as if the whole thing were her idea alone.

Or at least her and Mama's.

Merrilee wiped a glob of sauce from the corner of her mouth and studied the Reys. Nora sat straight as the principal, Mrs. Beecham, leafing through her salad as though she were looking for something in

✳ ✳ ✳

particular. Steven dug into his hamburger with gusto, caught Merrilee's eye, and winked. "You can ask those questions anytime," he said.

She smiled. He wasn't much like any of Mama's boyfriends, though some were nice enough. He didn't look at her like he wanted her to get lost or at least fetch something for him, like a pack of cigarettes or a cold beer from the fridge. Yet Steven Rey wanted more from her than anyone had ever asked—this baby, the only thing on earth she had to give, the last thing she wanted to part with.

"Uh . . . well, now I've forgotten what the book said," she said, angry that she'd lost the questions she'd worked to remember.

Nora laid down her fork. Her school-principal expression cracked, and her whole face seemed to open up like a moss rose to sunlight. "Speak from your heart," she said softly. "Let's forget about the book—all of us."

"Well, okay." Merrilee knew the questions she really wanted answered, but the book—and the Reys—would probably label them as too childish for a pregnant girl to ask. *Will you love my baby? Will you teach her to swim so she won't be afraid of the water? Will you take her to see* Sesame Street on Ice *and the circus and the rodeo, but will you also hold her hand and keep her from going places where she shouldn't, no matter how old she is?*

"How long have you been married?" she heard herself say and knew that the book's advice hadn't strayed too far from her.

"Twenty-three years," Nora said. "We met at the University of Texas and married right after we graduated from college. Steven went on to medical school, and I eventually got my real estate license."

"So schooling would be important to you?" Merrilee stuffed a bite of hamburger into her mouth, wishing that her heart could truly speak for her head. She already knew the answer. She already knew all the surface answers these people would give. They were meant to be parents. They would be good parents.

"Education is very important to us," Nora said.

"So you won't be working anymore?"

"No. I'll give up my job just as soon as we have a baby."

Merrilee knew Nora hadn't particularly meant her as part of that "we," that she meant any baby they might adopt. But she knew in her heart they were talking about her child, that the moment she was born, the Reys' life would forever change. And so would her own.

She set down her half-eaten hamburger, sud-

* * *

denly no longer hungry. Her hand rested on her stomach, and the baby kicked. Nora's eyes caught the movement, and she glanced at Steven, who had seen it too. A brief expression of love passed between them, and they clasped hands. They beamed at Merrilee, who suddenly felt like the stray cat she'd adopted long ago.

"I fixed up a box for her like you said, Mama. When will she have the kittens?"

Mama studied the box where Merrilee had set it, smack-dab in the middle of the trailer's living room. The cat kept trying to escape the box, and Merrilee just as persistently pressed her back in. "Move the box to the back of my closet, Merrilee, where it's nice and dark. Then leave her alone, hear? Don't be hovering over her. She wants a little peace and quiet while she does her thing without us bothering her."

"But I want to watch the kittens being born!"

Mama shook her head, putting a sympathetic arm around her daughter. "She'll know just what to do, darlin'. God gave her the instinct to be a mama, and that's just what we're going to leave her to do."

* * *

"Education's real important," Merrilee said to the couple who wanted her baby. Her mouth felt dry and raw as a broken chicken bone, and she sipped from her Sprite. She knew Nora was still studying her, and she wanted to slink under the table so her belly wouldn't be stared at anymore.

"What about you?" Nora said. "Do you plan to go back to school after your baby's born?"

You're darn right it's my baby, she wanted to say, then caught the sympathy in Nora's eyes. This woman was getting under her skin. Just when Merrilee wanted to dislike her for coveting her baby, Nora went and asked a nice question.

"I guess I'll finish school," she said.

"And after that?" Nora persisted, but still in that nice, calm tone.

Merrilee hadn't had much time to think about what she'd do after the baby was born and gone, but she did know instinctively she'd have to keep busy. "If Miss Ponds will hire me permanent at the library, I guess I'll become a full-time clerk."

"Did you ever think about going to college? To study to become a librarian, instead of just a clerk."

Merrilee licked her lips. "Yeah, I've thought about it. But I don't guess I'll have the money."

"There're always scholarships and grants,"
Steven put in. "At least think about it. Look
into it."

Merrilee shrugged. College was out of her
future. Working at the library would be a good
enough life. Certainly better than Mama'd had it,
working at the café, living off the tips she hoarded in
a jar. Surely after a while, people would forget about
the past. At least once she graduated from school in a
couple of years. Until then, the boys would no doubt
be after her all the time.

"Where will you go after the baby's born?"
Nora said. "Aren't you too young to live by yourself?"

Oh, if Nora Rey only knew. She'd been too
young for so long, but she'd been forced to be the
adult for more years than she could remember. She'd
done more than her share of cooking and cleaning,
even taking over the management of the tiny bank
account when she was twelve.

"I don't know," she said, hoping they'd leave off
asking about her and stick to the subject of the baby.
She crossed her arms defensively.

Nora noticed the action and leaned back, setting
space between them. "I'm sorry if I pried, Merrilee.
It's none of my business."

❋ ❋ ❋

Merrilee didn't reply, but she relaxed her arms. Nora just seemed concerned. Merrilee would have to watch that, or she'd let down her guard too quickly, too easily. Best the Reys not know the whole truth about things.

"Miss Ponds said I could move in with her," she said, tossing the couple a bone to throw them off the scent. "Look, I know what the book said. You've got every right to worry that I'm going to change my mind and keep this baby. I've got several strikes against me—I was raised by a single mother, I'm only fifteen, and I don't have any immediate plans. But I ain't going to change my mind, so just rest easy. Focus on the baby."

Your baby. Not mine.

They nodded, and Merrilee settled back against the vinyl booth. She focused on the dancing chili pepper again until the wetness in her eyes dried away.

❋❋❋❋❋❋❋❋❋❋❋❋❋❋❋❋❋❋❋❋❋❋❋

> *Dear Baby Girl,*
> *I met your parents today. Their names are Steven and Nora Rey, but you know that, by the time you're reading this. They're wonderful*

* * *

people, and I know you're going to be happy with them, as happy as I was growing up with Mama.

The Bible says lots of good things. Honor your father and mother, for one. I always tried to do that with my mama, and I know you will too. Steven and Nora will be different, though. They'll have money for you. Which can't buy happiness, everybody knows, but Mama used to say it could sure put a down payment on it. The rest was up to the man who held the mortgage.

Be happy no matter what you do, Baby Girl. My mama taught me that. There were lots of folks who resented her happiness because of who and what she was, as if her life was the reason for her joy. I knew it wasn't. I saw her cry time and again when some fella would stick around for a while and things would be good for both her and me. Then he'd leave and her heart would be broken yet again. Until that last time, she'd cry for a night, then be her old self the next day. "Joy comes in the morning, Merrilee. Don't the Bible say so?"

* * *

Steven and Nora will bring you joy all the time, Baby Girl, and not just because of their money. Steven's a real nice guy—I can tell. He'll treat you right and look out for you. He'll make sure the boys act decent and don't take advantage. And Nora—well, she seems a bit icy, but she's got a good heart deep down, I know. She wants you, doesn't she?

And if she wants you, I hope she wants me, even if it's only until it's time for you to be born. I could use a little wanting, myself.

Three

Nora had thought she'd be all talk after dropping Merrilee off. There was certainly much to discuss, but Nora wanted to keep private her thoughts about the girl. She was an absolute enigma, but Nora felt drawn, uncertain whether it was because of the baby or Merrilee herself.

Back at the house, Steven leaned against the door from the garage and studied her. "Didn't you like Merrilee?"

"Yes, of course," Nora said, startled by the question. "Why do you ask?"

"You barely said three words once we left Chili's and nothing since we dropped her back at Adoption Lifeline."

Nora sank into the butter-soft white leather sofa that overlooked the lake. Steven loosened his tie and sat on the bench of the Steinway angled in front of the tall windows. He looked down at the keys, but Nora knew he was watching her just the same, waiting in his own idle way. He launched into "Clair de Lune," and Nora blinked. The piece always brought her deepest emotions to the surface.

"She's so young," Nora said. "Some of my friends have daughters her age."

"It's ironic that a girl can get pregnant so easily." His hands skimmed over the keys.

"Yes. But she seems very mature about it all. I think that's what worries me."

Steven stopped playing and turned to face her. "That she'll change her mind?"

"She's fifteen, Steven. Girls that age change their mind as frequently as their clothes."

"Not Merrilee. She's different."

"Yes," Nora said, "but I thought more of what she didn't say than what she did."

"Do you think she's hiding something?"

"I'm not sure." Nora paused, trying to articulate
what intuition had been whispering ever since dinner.
"She seemed pretty unmoved about the baby's father
dying. Was he just one in a string of sexual partners?
Is she promiscuous?"

"Does it matter?"

Taken aback, Nora felt ashamed. "Why, no. It
shouldn't. That just came out. What an awful thing
for me to say."

He crossed his arms. "Is anything else that she
didn't say bothering you?"

"I'd like to know what happened to her mother,
even if it isn't our business to ask. I'd like to know
how that affected her."

"Seems to me she would have talked about that
if she wanted to."

Nora considered for a moment. "She was so
direct about other issues—reading, an education—but
when it came to questions about her future plans . . ."

"So she doesn't want to talk about herself."

"Still . . ." Nora trailed off, looking away.
Merrilee's silence seemed amazingly mature, yet still,
perhaps, a cover. Maybe she'd checked out the Reys
and found them lacking.

Steven sat beside her on the sofa and took her

hand. "We have two months until the baby's born. Why don't you get to know her some more? After all, you'll both be the mother of the baby, each in your own way."

"Oh, Steven, what am I supposed to do? Call her up and say, 'Hi there, Merrilee, let's bond'?"

"She probably just wants to be included a bit. To be seen as a person, not as a baby breeder. Why don't you meet on neutral ground? What do women like to do together?"

Nora grinned. "Talk about men."

Steven patted her knee and rose. "You'll think of something."

❋❋❋❋❋❋❋❋❋❋❋❋❋❋❋❋❋❋❋❋❋❋

"I'm glad you could meet me for shopping this afternoon," Nora said, glancing back and forth between Highway 360 traffic and Merrilee in the passenger seat. "I was afraid you might be busy."

Merrilee had the oddest feeling that Nora Rey was keeping tabs on her, so she stared straight ahead, her hand gripping the armrest. "Well, I wasn't doing much. Mrs. Pennywood said swimming's good exercise for me and the baby, so I went to the pool. But after that, there wasn't much to do but read."

❋ ❋ ❋

"Oh? Reading anything in particular?"

Merrilee shrugged. "I picked through some old books Mrs. Pennywood has in the bookcases. I read a little bit of *Gone with the Wind,* but I got bored. I've read it five times already."

"I haven't read that book in years." Nora smiled. "My mother took me to see the movie when I was about nine, and I was hooked. I probably read it five times before I was thirteen, myself."

"No kidding?" Merrilee loosened her hand from the armrest. "What else did you like to read when you were growing up?"

"The Little House on the Prairie books were probably my favorite. How about you?"

"Those were all right." Merrilee turned toward Nora. "I liked a little more adventure in my stories. Something like Nancy Drew. I'm still on the lookout for a few I haven't read yet."

"You mean you know the titles?"

"I even know the numbers of the ones under a hundred," Merrilee said proudly. "Twenty-four, twenty-six, twenty-nine, thirty-two, thirty-seven, thirty-eight, thirty-nine, forty-one, forty—"

"You can remember all those? I know grown women who can barely remember their own telephone numbers."

"Yep. I've been looking for them for so long, I got 'em memorized. There's twenty-six books in all, but like I said, those are just the numbers under a hundred. I have everything above that written in the back of my journal."

"How charming. I kept a diary too when I was a girl."

"No, ma'am, not a diary. A journal. Seems like there's a difference to me, though I'm not sure how to explain it. A journal seems kind of more grown-up somehow."

Nora deftly exited the highway and headed down a major street. The shops looked swanky, Merrilee noticed.

"Lots of women pay good money to learn how to journal," Nora said.

"I just write what I'm thinking about." Merrilee paused. "Actually, I wrote in it just for me the past year, but lately I've been writing in it for the baby."

"How sweet."

Merrilee drew a deep breath. "I got to be honest, Miz Rey. I'm not sure if I'll be able to give up that journal. I mean, to the baby, after she's born."

"Why?"

Merrilee glanced out her side window. "There's a lot of stuff that's probably only meant for me and

God to know. I write stuff for the baby, but by the time she's old enough to read it and understand what I'm saying, she probably won't want to know such things about her birth mama."

"She'll always wonder about you," Nora said. "She may even ask you herself . . . if you choose to stay in contact."

Merrilee heard the hesitation in Nora's voice. Did the thought of staying in touch pain her as much as it did Merrilee? "I don't see how I could."

Nora pulled into the parking lot of a fancy-looking store named Chez Les Enfants and found a spot near the entrance. She shut off the engine and looked at Merrilee, who suddenly felt like a bug under a microscope. To her surprise, Nora smiled warmly. "I don't want to make things difficult for you. We don't have to shop for baby things if you don't feel like it," she said.

Clothes that I'll never get to see the baby wear. Blankets I'll never get to cover her with.

Merrilee shrugged off such thoughts as self-pity. "Just seems natural. I sure can't afford to buy anything."

Nora kept looking at her as they got out of the car, and Merrilee regretted her hasty words. Did Nora think she was fishing for presents? They'd read the

✳ ✳ ✳

same adoption book after all, and it clearly warned
that some birth mothers tried to get as much as they
could from the adoptive parents. She'd tried not to
act like a gold digger at their first meeting, but maybe
Nora was afraid that now that they were alone,
Merrilee's true colors would show.

The door chimed the opening line of "Frère
Jacques" when they entered. Everything was pristine
and beautiful—baby clothes, toys, accessories—even
the diaper pails looked top-of-the-line and expensive.

Merrilee hung back, ducking her head.

"What's wrong?" Nora whispered.

"This place is really fancy," she whispered back,
raising her eyes, then lowering them again. An
expensively tailored saleswoman eyed Merrilee in her
cutoff shorts, leather sandals, and men's T-shirt with
the chopped-off sleeves. The saleswoman's face regis-
tered a mixture of amusement and dismay.

What had she been thinking? This wasn't Wal-
Mart. She should have dressed nicer. Nora was probably ashamed of her.

Nora caught the saleswoman's eye and give her
a disapproving look. She put an arm around Merrilee
and steered her toward the back, where the cribs and
bedding were displayed.

Merrilee ran her hand over a bright red chrome

✳ ✳ ✳

crib and gawked at the price tag. Mama would have swooned. "Uh . . . do you and Steven have a bed for the baby yet?"

Nora's expression suddenly looked like someone's who had been punched in the gut but was trying not to let it show. "I bought a crib about seven years ago. It was a really good sale, a beautiful crib." She paused. "We've never had a chance to assemble it."

"Oh," Merrilee said. *What a stupid thing for me to ask.* "What does it look like?" she said, feeling that if she dropped the subject it would simply fester.

"Are you familiar with the Jenny Lind style?"

Merrilee shook her head.

"It's old-fashioned looking—curvy spindles all around the bed. Here, see? There's one just like it, although the one we have is white."

Merrilee stroked the top rail, smiling. "White would be pretty for a girl. This is a nice design. I kinda like old-fashioned–looking things for babies— not all this bright-colored stuff. That's more for kids who can run around and have fun. Babies need soft, quiet colors."

She touched the Mickey and Minnie Mouse mobile hanging above the crib and gave the music box a quick turn. "When You Wish upon a Star" sounded, and the characters danced above the empty

✳ ✳ ✳

bed. Merrilee blinked, her throat tightening. "I really like lullabies. Have you bought one of these things yet?"

"No, we haven't." Nora stepped closer. "What do you think the baby would like?"

Merrilee glanced away. Such things were not for her to think about. "I don't know, Miz Rey. Seems like that's your call."

"Please call me Nora." She paused. "We can leave if you'd like. But if it's not too painful, I really would appreciate your opinion."

"Miz Rey . . . Nora," she amended, without looking up, "I told you and your husband that I'm not going to change my mind. You don't have to be nice to me because you're afraid I might."

"I'm not. Steven and I will accept whatever you decide. But if you choose us to raise your baby, I want you to have as much say as you desire. And that includes what the baby wears and what mobile she looks at." Nora hesitated. "If you want to help."

"It's painful for me." Merrilee drew a deep breath. "But probably no more than it is for you. Coming to a baby store like this, I mean. It must have been hard to look at this stuff for all these years, knowing you couldn't have your own baby."

Nora smiled. "You're very perceptive. What do

* * *

you say we get out of here? The baby stuff can wait. Would you like to come to my house?"

"Are you sure you want me there? I know the book says you may not want me to know your address. In case I start bugging you guys after the baby's born or something."

"Why would I not want you to see where your baby's going to live? We can stop by Adoption Lifeline and pick up your swimsuit and a change of clothes. Let's make a day of it. Steven's at work—it'll be just us girls."

Merrilee couldn't respond. How close did she want to get to this woman?

Nora studied her. "You said yourself you didn't have anything to do. Besides, if you get tired of hanging with me, Steven and I have lots of books. Some of my old copies of Nancy Drew are on the shelves. I like a little adventure myself, some days."

Merrilee grinned, feeling bashful. It *had* been a spell since she'd had a good time. "Okay. It sounds like fun."

✳✳✳✳✳✳✳✳✳✳✳✳✳✳✳✳✳✳✳✳✳✳✳

She's just interested in the baby. She's just interested in the baby. Merrilee repeated the words all the way out to

✳ ✳ ✳

Nora's house. She tried to focus on the hills west of town, tried to soak in the memory of the scrubby terrain and cedars standing guard over shimmering Lake Travis. She wanted to tell Sylvie Ponds all about the scenery later, but she was too unnerved by the woman behind the wheel of the fancy Lincoln Navigator.

When they pulled into the driveway of the Reys' home, Merrilee was even more unnerved. "Wow," she said, licking her lips as the gate swung closed behind them and the large house loomed in front. "You guys must be really rich."

Nora parked the SUV in the garage, and Merrilee was out of the Navigator like buckshot, racing around the side of the house to check out the view. She clutched the paper bag holding her swimsuit and change of clothes.

They live on the lake! And a pool! Why would anyone have a pool when this gorgeous lake is right here? It's so—

A dog barked, and Merrilee pulled up just shy of the pool area. A large German shepherd bounded toward her, and she screamed. Dropping the bag, she raced back toward the garage, her heart pounding madly. Barking louder, the dog gave chase. Merrilee's eyes filled with tears, and she ran straight into Nora Rey.

* * *

Nora put her arms around her. "It's all right, Merrilee. He's harmless. Really. Lucky! Down!"

Closing her eyes, Merrilee snuggled into Nora's arms. The dog quieted, and Merrilee sensed that he had stopped a good distance away.

"Good boy," Nora said, in an even, friendly tone. "This is Merrilee. She's my friend, and you scared her. I think you should apologize."

Merrilee opened her eyes. She couldn't believe this woman was talking to a dog like a person. She also couldn't believe she'd thrown herself at Nora Rey like a little kid. She peered around to make sure Lucky was still "down." The dog laid on the grass, looking up at her, panting . . . salivating . . . as though she were a choice piece of prime rib.

"There, you see?" Nora said to her. "He's really a nice dog. Just overly exuberant."

Merrilee eased away from Nora but stayed close. "Can we go in the house now? He stays outside, doesn't he?"

Nora laughed. "Most of the time. On an occasional stormy night, we let him in." She patted Merrilee's shoulder, then, as if realizing the intimacy of the action, cleared her throat. "Head for the front door. I'll get your bag and make sure Lucky has enough water. Then I'll be right in. Here's the key."

Merrilee held the rest of the keys on the ring
in the palm of her hand and held out the house key
between her thumb and forefinger. What if she
dropped the key ring and all the keys got mixed up?
Nora had so many.

To her relief, she managed to get the door open.
She quietly shut it behind her, catching her breath
with a little gulp in her throat.

The house was gorgeous. Spotless. Beautiful.
A wide-open "sittin' area," as Mama would have
called it, with large, smooth ceramic floor tiles; deep,
cushiony furniture and glass tables; several tall, green,
leafy plants in gleaming gold pots; bookcases filled
with books; and a big black piano situated by the
most wonderful view Merrilee had ever seen.

Everything she'd ever want in a home, mostly
because it overlooked the lake with tall glass panes.
She could curl up by those windows in that rattan
chair with the big cushion and dream the day away.
She'd read a little, maybe sipping on some iced tea,
then glance up from her book and stare out those
windows, watching the world. Why, with a view
like this, they could probably find a cure for all
those terminal diseases and solve world peace! They
should fly in scientists and world leaders to this very
spot. All the answers in the world were right out

* * *

there, hovering over the lake, right within reach,
she was sure.

Merrilee shook her head. She'd have to remember to write about this in the journal tonight. To tell
her baby that when she felt sad or lonely or needed
some answers, all she'd have to do is sit by those
windows and do some praying. She could imagine
her sitting there as a young girl with long hair, deep
in thought, worried over some childish thing. Nora
would kneel and put an arm around her. "What's
wrong, sweetheart?" she'd say. "What can I help
you with?"

Nora would be good at that. She'd be good as a
mother. Sympathetic. Maybe that's because she liked
to read. Mama wasn't very good at knowing when
Merrilee was upset or hurting, but then she didn't
ever get into books much. She always said she was
too busy living her life to stick her nose in some old
book, the way Merrilee did.

Yes, it would be Nora Rey who comforted
Merrilee's Baby Girl.

"Nora," she whispered to herself firmly.

"Goodness, Merrilee." Nora had opened the
front door without Merrilee hearing. "Don't you
want to sit down?"

"I was kind of afraid to. Everything's so nice."

✳ ✳ ✳

Nora smiled, laying her purse on the kitchen counter, then setting Merrilee's paper bag beside it. "Have a seat, and I'll fix us some lemonade. Whew. It's like a steam bath outside." She fanned herself, and the loose blonde hairs that framed her face rose up and fell back into perfect place. "You must be really hot. Let's have our lemonade, and then we can go swimming."

"That sounds good." Merrilee glanced around the living room. "Can I sit anywhere?"

Nora smiled. "Anywhere you'd like."

Merrilee headed straight for the big-cushioned rattan chair by the window. It was tough to tuck her legs underneath her, Indian-style, but she finally managed. She felt like she was inside a cushioned bowl tilted sideways, secure and enclosed like the baby who danced inside her.

Merrilee glanced at the doorway and saw that Nora was still puttering in the kitchen. She put her hands on her belly and smiled. "It's a great place to sit, isn't it, Baby Girl? I wish you could see the view from my side of things. The lake's real blue and calm, and there're birds flying around out there on the rocks."

She looked around the room. "If I was you and I got tired of looking out these windows or reading

all those books—though I don't think I ever could—
I'd sit at that piano. I don't know how to play anything, but I'd sure learn. It's a beautiful piano, Baby
Girl. Black and shiny. A grand piano, I think. Maybe
a baby grand."

Merrilee rubbed her belly wistfully, and her
voice dropped to a whisper. "A baby grand for a
grand baby. I hope you learn how to play."

"Merrilee, wouldn't you like to sit over here?"
Nora nodded at the plush L-shaped sectional sofa,
then handed Merrilee a tall glass of lemonade. "It's
much more comfortable than that old papasan chair."

"A *what* chair?"

"Papasan."

"Oh. Well, it's fine." She snuggled in. "Real
cozy. Where'd you get it?"

Nora sat at the far end of the sofa. "It was the
first piece of furniture Steven and I bought together,
when we were newlyweds. It wasn't very expensive,
but we had to buy it on time." She smiled, remembering. "Oh, how we dreaded those payments! I
haven't had the heart to get rid of that chair, even
though it's seldom used anymore. We keep it for
sentimental value."

"Because you're doing so well now?" Merrilee
felt her ears burn, and she sipped from the lemonade

✳ ✳ ✳

to cover her embarrassment. That was probably a
rude thing to say. Mama said you shouldn't make
mention of a person's money—whether he obviously
had too little or plenty to spare.

The question didn't seem to bother Nora,
though. "Having money isn't everything."

"It doesn't hurt." Merrilee glanced around the
room.

Nora set her lemonade on the glass coffee table.
"I don't keep the chair to remind us of how well
we've done financially, but how we've overcome
many struggles since those early days. Just like we
knew we'd eventually pay off that chair, I've always
believed we'll conquer all the obstacles that get
thrown our way in marriage."

"Like not being able to have your own baby?"
Merrilee immediately glanced down. "I didn't
mean to blurt that out. I'm always talking without
thinking."

Nora moved down the sofa, closer to Merrilee.
"It's all right to mention it. Yes, one of our struggles
has been my infertility."

"Oh." Merrilee stared out over the water. Did
Nora ever want to just get on a boat and ride away
from shore, ride, ride, until she was far away from her
problems?

* * *

Probably not. A woman like Nora probably coped well with her problems.

Still, Merrilee felt awkward sitting in this show house, awkward and fat and blessed in a way Nora would never be. It didn't seem right that she'd gotten a child the way she had, while Nora'd probably tried and tried for years with no success. She wanted to feel angry at her, for wanting the one thing Merrilee herself wanted above all else, but all she could find in her heart was a desire to help.

"You're a very observant girl," Nora said. "I noticed that at the baby store. It was nice of you to think about my discomfort when that saleswoman was obviously giving you a negative once-over."

Merrilee shrugged. "I'm used to it, though I never really noticed it until it was obvious I was carrying a baby. Most of Palmwood treated me like that. Mama too."

"What happened to your mother?"

Merrilee squirmed in the chair. She shouldn't have come here. She wished Nora had just showed her the baby's room and every place she'd be, then driven Merrilee back to the safety of Adoption Lifeline. People didn't ask questions there. Nora wasn't asking in a prying way, but she was asking all the same.

"If it's rude of me to have asked, don't feel you have to answer."

The trouble was, Merrilee didn't have the ability to lie. Mama'd raised her not to, even when it hurt to tell the truth.

"I don't guess it's rude of you to ask about Mama," she said slowly. "After all, you'll be raising her grandbaby."

Merrilee felt tears at the back of her eyes, and she turned to the window. She was not going to blow it right here in the Reys' house, in this comfy chair, blow any chance for a good life for her baby. She turned back to Nora, steadying her voice. "Mama killed herself."

Nora's expression shifted from cool blandness to disbelief. "Oh, Merrilee—"

"It's okay." Merrilee drew a deep breath. *One, two, three . . . don't let her see.* "I've had about a month to get over it."

"A month isn't much time," Nora said gently, perching on the edge of the sofa. She looked like she wanted to say something, but instead she clasped her hands together tightly.

"The time's gone by real fast." Merrilee drew another deep breath and smiled. "And now I'm here.

* * *

Well, not like I'm living at your house or anything, but here in Austin."

The front door swung open, and Lucky leaped into the room. "Hey, Blondie!" Steven called. "Where ya hiding?"

Merrilee shrieked as Lucky headed straight for her. Tail wagging, he put his front paws on her knee. Merrilee cowered, arms protecting her face as she drew her legs up to protect the baby. "Shoo! Go away! Bad dog!"

"Lucky, down!" Nora said in sharp command. "Steven, come get Lucky."

"Merrilee!" Steven stopped short by the piano. "I didn't expect to see you here. Is Lucky bothering you?"

"Y-yes!" She hid her face in her arms.

"She doesn't like big dogs," Nora said, grasping Lucky's collar firmly. She gave the shepherd a stern look. "Especially big, enthusiastic dogs."

Lucky ducked his head, as if he knew he was in trouble. He glanced at Merrilee and whined. Merrilee kept her face covered.

"I'll take him." Steven took him from Nora and headed outside.

Merrilee lowered her arms when she heard the door close.

✳ ✳ ✳

"You're safe," Nora said, her voice sounding like a smile. "Is there any special reason you're afraid of big dogs?"

Another question. Nora Rey was pressing hard. She hesitated, then decided the story wasn't too revealing. "When I was little, one of my mama's boy-friends had a big dog—a rottweiler, I think it was. We never went to Mama's boyfriends' houses, but Mama said he owed her money and we'd had a lean week. She said he couldn't refuse her the money if he saw her little girl. We knocked politely on the door, but he didn't answer, even though his pickup truck was outside."

Merrilee shifted in the chair. "Then Mama pounded on the door, yelling 'bout how he owed her and did he want her little girl to starve. The door opened, and this big old dog came charging out, barking, teeth bared. He went for me 'cause I was smaller than Mama, I guess, and he tore a chunk of skin loose from between my eyes before Mama whacked him with her purse."

"What happened then?"

She shrugged. "All I remember is seeing blood and wondering if that old dog had ripped my eyes out, then the sound of a rifle and the man swearing up and down to my screaming Mama that he didn't mean us no harm and he'd pay for any medical bills."

She paused. "I got stitched up and we lived pretty good for a few weeks after that. We never saw that fellow again, though. Not long after, he moved away from Palmwood."

Nora cleared her throat. "I'm sorry about Lucky. He wouldn't hurt a fly, but I can see why you'd be afraid of him. I'll keep him away from you."

"Thanks."

"Feel like that swim now?"

Merrilee glanced out over the pool and saw Lucky chasing a bird. "Um, I don't think so."

Steven entered. "So did you ladies find anything at the baby stores?"

Nora and Merrilee looked at each other. "We didn't shop long," Nora said.

"Nora told me about the crib you have for the baby, though," Merrilee said, trying to make conversation. "It sounds pretty."

"Would you like to see it?" Nora said. "It's in the room we'll use as a nursery."

"Sure." Getting the conversation back to the baby made Merrilee feel on safer, firmer ground. She rose and followed Nora and Steven as they led the way down a carpeted hallway.

* * *

"We haven't decorated yet," Nora said, flipping on the room's light switch. "Right now it's still just a guest room."

Merrilee smiled. The room was light and airy, with wispy white curtains and furniture. Several watercolor paintings of old-fashioned–looking women and plump babies decorated the cream-colored walls.

"A friend of mine painted those," Nora said proudly. "She has five children, and each one was a model."

No wonder they're in the guest room. Nora's probably proud of her friend's work, but it must be an awful reminder that she can't have kids. "They're nice," Merrilee said, wishing she'd never looked at them in the first place. The cherubic children made her feel not only bad for Nora but bad for herself as well. The women in the paintings probably had husbands in the background, as a real family should.

"Here we go." Steven lugged out the crib's four unassembled sides from a closet and held them out for inspection.

Nora blew on the dust, then wiped it with her hand, which came away grimy. "We'd take some soap and water to it before we set it up, of course," she said to Merrilee.

She nodded, touching the dirty rails with awe.

I'll never get to see you sleeping here, Baby Girl. But at least I know you'll have a nice bed.

Nora cleared her throat lightly. "Thanks, Steven. Merrilee, I didn't mean to keep you so long. Are you ready to head back to Adoption Lifeline?"

Merrilee nodded, not sure of her voice, not sure of much of anything anymore.

Four

Nora pulled the covers up to her shoulders and turned on her side, watching Steven brush his teeth in the bathroom just beyond their bedroom. He hummed while he rinsed the toothbrush, then washed his face.

She rolled onto her back, squeezing her eyes shut. What had Merrilee thought about the father of her baby? She'd never expressed any affection for him, even though he was apparently dead. Had she

＊ ＊ ＊

loved him, in her own teenage way, as Nora loved Steven? Had she allowed him to take liberties in a vain attempt to keep him at her side?

Why had her mother killed herself? *Oh, Merrilee!*

"You've been quiet all evening again," Steven said. He flicked off the table lamp, plunging the room into moonlight. He slipped under the covers beside her.

Instantly she moved into his arms, seeking comfort. "Do you know how Merrilee's mother died?" Nora's eyes filled with tears. "She killed herself, Steven. Imagine a girl that age, pregnant, unmarried, and her mother commits suicide. Then she brings herself here, to Austin, to let us adopt her baby."

"You'd never know from talking to her that she carried such burdens. She's more levelheaded than most adults I know."

"Yes, but she—" Nora broke off, remembering how Merrilee had stared out their window, rubbing her belly. The maternal act had stopped Nora short in the kitchen, unwilling to intrude. She'd seen Merrilee's lips moving, as though she was speaking to the baby. Nora didn't think she'd ever seen love and compassion register so openly on someone's face, yet mixed with such impending sorrow. She'd realized then, watching Merrilee curled into the old papasan

* * *

chair, that she and Steven would be taking from the
girl that which she loved most.

"I want to help her," Nora said, pressing her
cheek against her husband's bare chest. "She's so
young, and she's all alone."

"We're going to help her by raising her baby."

"But then what happens to her? Is she going to
go back to being a clerk at that small-town library,
struggling to get her high school diploma? What kind
of life will she lead? Who'll take care of her?"

"Probably the librarian—Sylvie Ponds, I think
she said her name was."

"But what will Merrilee do with the rest of her
life? She's such an intelligent, compassionate girl. I
can't let her just walk into our lives, place her baby
in our arms, then let her walk away! Is that what God
wants from us?"

Steven was silent for a moment. "Perhaps I was
wrong in suggesting that you two get to know each
other better."

Nora sat up. "Steven Rey, are you saying you
don't care that her mother committed suicide just a
month ago? that she's never known a father herself?
How can you be so callous?"

"Of course I care, Nora." Steven laid his hand
on her arm. "But I care more about you. And I don't

want to see your heart broken yet again, like it has every month, every year since we first decided to have children."

"You said if it was God's will that we have children, that we would," she said in a low voice. "You said to have faith. Everybody said to have faith. And now it looks like we're finally going to get a baby. Who's going to have faith for Merrilee? Is she just supposed to swim upstream, spawn, then disappear from our lives? from our hearts?" Her voice caught on a sob.

"Nora, Nora." Steven eased her back down beside him, into the comfort of his arms. "Shh. It'll be all right. Once the baby's born, it'll all work out. You'll see. We'll be busy with the baby, and Merrilee's life will go on. Have faith. It'll all work out."

Steven kissed her temples and cheeks. Nora closed her eyes and asked for such faith, asked for direction at this juncture of her and Merrilee's paths.

* *

The next two weeks proved almost as nerve-wracking to Nora as the multitude of preceding years she and Steven had tried to get pregnant.

* * *

He convinced her not to contact Merrilee, to wait until they heard from her first.

"Mrs. Pennywood's told us she's fine. We've courted her, Nora," he said one morning at breakfast, when she wondered aloud why they hadn't heard from Merrilee herself. "We don't want to push the situation. We've made our desire for her baby clear."

"So has she," Nora said. "She assured us that she wasn't going to change her mind. What's the harm in spending time with her?"

"The harm might be to you if she does change her mind. The baby isn't ours until she signs the papers." Steven folded up the *Austin American–Statesman*. "Time for me to go to the office. How about you?"

Nora shook her head, swallowing from her coffee mug to hide the betraying expression certainly etched across her face. "I'm not handling any hot properties at the moment, so I'm not going in today. I have some things to do, errands to run, that sort of thing."

He kissed her and smiled as he headed for the garage. "I'll call later. Love you!"

"Love you too!"

The minute she heard the Lexus back out of the garage, she went to her room to change clothes.

* * *

87

✳✳✳✳✳✳✳✳✳✳✳✳✳✳✳✳✳✳✳✳✳✳✳✳✳

Merrilee couldn't believe she was riding with Nora Rey again and especially that they were driving back to the woman's house. "I was surprised to hear from you, Nora," she said.

"Why is that?"

Merrilee shrugged. "I figured you'd met me and that'd be it. Until the baby's born, that is. Mrs. Pennywood says that's the way it is with most adoptive parents and birth mothers."

"She didn't advise you against meeting with me again, did she?"

Merrilee paused. "She said that if we're going to keep meeting, we should agree now on what's going to happen after the baby's born."

"You mean as to how involved you'll be in the baby's life?"

Merrilee nodded. "She said that if we don't set the ground rules now, we could all be in for a lot of hurt later."

"Then we can discuss that when Steven gets home from work," Nora said breezily, but Merrilee thought that a worried look briefly crossed her face. "Meanwhile . . . I owe you a swim in our pool,

✳ ✳ ✳

remember? I'll put Lucky inside, and we can enjoy
the outdoors. You brought your swimsuit?"

Merrilee nodded and held out a paper bag, identical to the one she'd brought before.

At the house, Nora ushered Merrilee into what
she called the guest room to change into her swimsuit. Merrilee changed quickly, fingers trembling as
she adjusted the straps.

She didn't feel right, lingering in the room, so
she found her way back to the living room, feeling
nervous. Her stomach seemed to pooch out even
more than usual, covered by the floppy blue maternity swimsuit. Long-lashed goldfish and much smaller
baby goldfish playfully chased across the material.

Nora entered the room in a sleek one-piece, and
Merrilee pointed at her own suit, trying to disguise
her embarrassment. "It's not exactly my style," she
said, "but it's all Mrs. Pennywood had to loan me."

"It's kind of cute, actually."

Merrilee shook her head. "Not like yours. Last
summer I had a tie-dyed bikini and a great tan.
Wayne said—" She broke off. "Well, that was last
summer."

Thankfully, Nora smiled and let the subject
drop. "Let me put Lucky in the laundry room. Then
we can go outside."

"He'll be okay, won't he? I mean, it's not like a small space or anything, is it?"

"He'll be a little unhappy, but I set out some food and water and his favorite blanket in there. He'll curl right up and go to sleep."

Merrilee felt relieved. Lucky scared the tar out of her, but he couldn't help that she was still a scaredy-baby about dogs.

Even though it was only the last week in May, the sun's heat glared off the concrete around the pool. Merrilee let Nora rub sunscreen on her back, and then she returned the favor.

"I hate this stuff, but I hate sunburn even worse," Merrilee said, slathering her nose. "Once I got really sick from a bad sunburn. I wouldn't want to do that while I'm carrying this baby."

At that moment, the baby jabbed like a prize-fighter, and Merrilee winced.

Nora stopped her own sunscreen application and stared. "What does that feel like?"

"What? Oh, the baby? Here. Feel for yourself."

She guided Nora's hand to her abdomen, and they were soon rewarded with another gymnastic maneuver.

Nora laughed. "She's really thrashing around! She's like one of those fish on your swimsuit."

* * *

Merrilee laughed too. "That's what she feels
like, all right. Like a big fish, whipping its tail
around."

Nora withdrew her hand, smiling at Merrilee.
"It must feel wonderful when you can feel it inside
you. You're so fortunate. So blessed."

Merrilee felt her smile slip involuntarily. "Yeah,
well, I don't know if 'blessing' applies to all this. It's
been more like a curse from my end of things. But
the blessing is that you're going to get a baby after
years of waiting, and my little girl will have a good
home."

"What about you, Merrilee? What would it take
to make you feel blessed?"

Nora's eyes were far too penetrating. Merrilee
had to look away, so she studied the lake. "I think . . .
if I could only go back in time about eight months."

"Before the baby was conceived?"

Merrilee swallowed, unable to answer. "Let's
get in the pool. It's hot."

Nora went straight to the deep end and dived in.
Merrilee sat on the pool steps, barely in the water.

Nora saw her and waved. "Come on in," she
said, treading water at the far end.

Merrilee eyed the water. "I just like to get my
feet wet."

✳ ✳ ✳

Nora swam to the shallow end. "Can you swim at all?"

"Not very well." Merrilee shuddered.

"You can float on your back, can't you?"

"I always sink. Especially now, with the baby."

"The extra weight won't matter in the water. Here, I'll help you. Stand up, here, on the bottom of the pool."

Something in Nora's voice reassured her, or maybe it was the gesture of her hands, like a mother beckoning her toddler. Merrilee walked down the remaining steps.

"Now walk out a bit more, about up to your waist."

Merrilee grinned. "I don't have a waist any-more."

"Then where it used to be." Nora smiled back, walking backward until the water encircled her own middle.

Merrilee complied.

"Put your arms out, lean back on the water, and let your feet rise till you're lying on your back. Imagine that you're stretching out on a bed. You never worry about a bed collapsing under you, do you?"

Merrilee did as Nora asked, and Nora placed her hands under Merrilee's back and knees, keeping her

* * *

straight. Her stomach stuck up toward the sun, like a precious offering.

"That's it, Merrilee. You can do it. That's it! Let the water hold you up. Now stay in this position."

Nora released her hands, and Merrilee stayed afloat. She grinned, waving her arms slowly through the water. Jubilant, she jumped upright, touched bottom, and flipped back her wet hair. "I did it!"

"Of course you did. You just needed a little help."

She felt confident, like she could swim to China. "I'm going to try it again."

Merrilee practiced floating, paddling happily around the pool. Nora swam slow laps around her, and Merrilee felt encircled, protected. At last Nora got out of the water and asked Merrilee if she was hungry.

"Starved!" said Merrilee happily, making her ungainly way up the pool steps. Water dripped in puddles around her, and Nora wrapped her in a thick, sun-warmed towel.

"I'll bring lunch out here," Nora said. "Have a seat under the umbrella at the table."

Merrilee felt warm and drowsy, happy and cared for. Nora brought out a tray of finger sandwiches and vegetables with dip, as well as plates and lemonade.

Merrilee dug in with gusto but stopped after a few bites. "What kind of sandwich is this?"

"Cucumber. If you don't like it, you don't have to eat it. There's peanut butter sandwiches on the tray too."

Merrilee chewed thoughtfully. "It's not bad." She chewed some more. "Pretty good, actually. Maybe you can show me how to make them. I like to fix new things."

"Do you like to cook?"

"Yes, ma'am. I cooked most of the meals for me and Mama since I was about ten years old. She worked at a café and hated the sight of food, so I figured I'd help her out some at home. Did most of the cleaning too." Merrilee stopped, ashamed that she'd prattled on for so long. "I guess you're tired of hearing about me and Mama. Our lives must seem pretty inferior compared to yours."

"You think mine is better?"

How could she even ask? "Yeah, I think your life is better. Look at this place. It's gorgeous. You've got a great husband, a job."

"Lives can't be measured by material possessions, Merrilee. That's not an indication of a person's success."

"No, probably not." Merrilee sipped her lemonade. "All I know is Mama wasn't a success by any

* * *

long shot, and she certainly didn't have anything except our broken-down old trailer."

"You were her greatest treasure, Merrilee," Nora said softly. "She had you."

"Yeah, she had me, all right. I used to think it was enough, just her and me, no matter how many men dumped her."

"Your mother had lots of boyfriends?"

Merrilee set down her lemonade. "Yeah. But they didn't stick around long. By the time I was nine, I knew they never would. But Mama kept on believing in that white knight who'd take care of us for the rest of our lives." She paused. "When this baby made her presence known, I figured it'd be enough to make Mama happy—me, her, and the baby."

Nora looked intrigued by this revelation. "You were going to keep the baby?"

Merrilee nodded, miserable. "Mama's death changed everything."

"I want to understand." Nora leaned forward. "I don't want to pry, but you're . . . you're . . ."

"Holding back?"

Nora started. "Those weren't exactly the words I'd expect someone your age to use, but yes. Holding back."

* * *

Merrilee glanced down at her hands. What could she say?

Nora looked disappointed that Merrilee hadn't confided in her, but she gamely passed the plate. "Here. Have another cucumber sandwich."

Merrilee knew instinctively that Nora wanted to break down her guard and gain her trust. What surprised Merrilee was the realization that she was beginning to want Nora Rey to succeed.

After some sunbathing time, Merrilee asked if she could get back in the water. She flat-out loved the Reys' pool. It was clean and clear, unlike the city pool at Palmwood, which usually looked about as clear as the nearest creek, the one that ran downstream from the concrete plant.

But even as she worked on floating again, Merrilee kept looking over her shoulder at the lake down the hill from the Reys' home. She felt greedy for wanting more, but it beckoned her, the sun glinting off the gentle waves, the bobbing buoys in the distance.

It was even better than the view from the Reys' windows, everything so close and big, like when, as a girl, she'd planted herself only two feet away from the TV to watch.

* * *

"Merrilee, you're going to ruin your eyes, sitting that close," Mama warned.

"No, I won't." Merrilee never took her eyes from the screen. The black-and-white sitcom was riveting, far removed from her life. "The eye doctor who came to my school for exams said it didn't matter."

"Them doctors. What do they know, anyhow?" Mama pulled deep on her cigarette, then tapped the ashes into her empty beer glass. "Well, I guess you're okay. Your teacher did send a note home that your eyes are fine. But that don't mean you can sit there all night. When Charley gets here, you're going to have to turn off that contraption, honey. I'll need you to play in your room for a while."

"Oh, Mama, again? Charley's been over here nearly every night this week. I can't watch any of my favorite shows anymore!"

"Never mind, Merrilee," Mama said, waving her cigarette. "He likes to come here and spend time with us—get away from that harpy he has for a wife."

"But, Mama, I want to spend time with just you. Can't you tell him not to come over tonight? I won't even ask to watch TV—

❋ ❋ ❋

*I promise! Maybe we could go get some ice cream
or play a board game."*

*"Not tonight." Mama massaged her tem-
ples, as if she had one of her sick headaches.
"Just remember that if we're good to Charley,
he'll be good to us."*

But he hadn't been, any more than any of them
had been. Especially the last one, Lucas Procter.

And his son, Wayne.

"Merrilee? You keep staring at the lake," Nora
said. "Would you like to walk down there?"

"Sure. It looks pretty from up here."

"There's a swing out at the boathouse in the
shade. If Steven were here, we could get him to take
us for a boat ride. I don't like to drive it myself."

"I can't blame you. I started learning to drive a
car, and I'm not in a big hurry. I figure I'll just keep
taking the bus around Palmwood. Leastways to places
where I can't walk."

She rubbed at her back with a knotted fist. "It
sure will be easier to do that when I'm not carrying
this baby anymore. The doctor I saw said she wasn't a
big baby, but she feels like a ton of bricks sometimes."

"Mrs. Pennywood said that the doctor thinks
everything's fine. Did he say anything else to you?"

✳ ✳ ✳

"Just to keep eating healthy. He scheduled one of those ultrasounds in two weeks." She ducked her head shyly. "Would you and Steven like to go with me?"

Nora smiled. "We'd be honored."

They walked down the tall stairway to the boat-house, Nora insisting on grabbing at Merrilee's arm every so often. "Are you sure you don't want to stop and rest?"

"I'm fine."

"What about going back up? Will you be able to make it?"

Merrilee grinned. "I guess women have been having babies and walking up steps for a lot longer than I've been pregnant. I'll make it. Nothing'll happen to this baby."

"I'm concerned about you too, Merrilee," Nora said.

Merrilee shrugged.

The boathouse was small, little more than a covered shed for waterskiing equipment and fishing tackle, but Merrilee thought it was grand. She wondered if the Reys would let her move in down here, where she could look out at the lake every day and keep an eye on her baby, growing up there on the hill above.

✳ ✳ ✳

Dejected, she slumped down on a double-seater redwood swing, attached to the roof with heavy chains. If she swung high and fast enough, she could launch herself out over the water into a crazy dive. The idea cheered her a little. Then she remembered that she'd better resist temptation for the baby's sake.

Nora sat beside her, and Merrilee stiffened. She liked the woman a lot, the way she liked Sylvie Ponds, but unlike Sylvie, Nora persisted with gentle questions that threatened Merrilee's defenses. Sylvie never asked anything. Merrilee was grateful for the privacy, but she sometimes wondered if maybe Sylvie just didn't have enough sense to realize what had happened. Apparently nobody in Palmwood did, which accounted for the cold shoulders she'd gotten since her pregnancy was obvious.

Especially since Mama died.

Merrilee studied a hummingbird feeder hanging at the edge of the roof. Two birds zipped in and out, their wings fluttering too quickly to be seen.

"Is your mama still alive?" Merrilee said abruptly. "Will my baby have grandparents?"

"Steven's parents live in Massachusetts. We visit each other at least twice a year. Steven's brother and sister each have two children, so his folks are experts at grandparenting. They're good at it too. Just enough spoiling to make a child feel special and plenty of good, solid loving."

Merrilee kicked her feet against the rough boards of the boathouse pier to set the swing in motion. "What about you?"

Nora absentmindedly set her end of the swing in rhythm with Merrilee, shading her eyes against the sun. "They're both dead. My father died when I was a teenager. My mother died just a few years ago."

"What of?"

"She had a stroke. It was a blessing, really, that she passed on."

Merrilee squinted. "Why would you say that?"

"The stroke incapacitated her. She couldn't speak, couldn't move one side of her body, even. She had to be spoon-fed her meals."

"At least she was still alive."

Nora pressed her feet against the swing, slowing its motion. "My mother was a huge perfectionist. Everything had to be perfect, just right, or life wasn't worth living."

Merrilee sat, thoughtful. "Must have been hard on you, though, when she passed. You have any brothers or sisters?"

Nora shook her head. "No, she just had me to keep in check for my whole life."

Merrilee laughed. "Keep you in check? No way! I bet you were the perfect kid."

"I tried, but it was never enough." Nora paused. "Even my not being able to get pregnant was a black mark against me."

"But you couldn't help that."

"I wish I'd been able to convince Mother of that. She wanted grandchildren so much. Not to play with and love, like most grandmothers, but as a showpiece. To prove that her daughter, Nora Templett Rey, wife of the stellar orthopedic surgeon, Steven Payne Rey, could perform the most basic biological feat—to be fertile."

"I think my mama was just the opposite," Merrilee said. "She didn't think I'd ever get pregnant."

"Was she angry when you told her? Did she know early on?"

Merrilee looked Nora dead in the eye. She wanted to say, *Stop pressing!* It hurt to talk this much, not because of what she was afraid she might reveal, but because of what she was afraid she wouldn't. Nora was actually interested—seemingly not for gossip's sake but out of concern.

For the baby, of course, you dummy. She wants to make sure Mama didn't beat me or anything, to cause any damage.

"She wasn't angry so much as disappointed," Merrilee said. "She knows better than anybody that single moms have it bad."

Mama just stared after Merrilee announced she'd taken a home pregnancy kit that came out positive. "Didn't you tell the boy to use something, Merrilee?" she said, shaking her head. She lit a cigarette and looked out the small, smudged window of the trailer's kitchen. "You told Wayne yet?"

"No, ma'am," she whispered. "I think he's moved out of town, anyway."

"You think?" Mama turned, her eyes like lava. "You chose to get cozy enough with a boy to be carrying his seed and you don't know where he is?"

"I haven't seen him in a fistful of weeks, Mama. Haven't you noticed he stopped coming around?"

Haven't you noticed that I'm glad, Mama? Haven't you noticed that I've been crying into my pillow every night? Didn't you even see that I was throwing up every morning? You probably could have told me what was wrong long before this cheap drugstore test!

"His daddy ain't been coming around neither," Mama said bitterly, squashing the cigarette in the sink. Her eyes spit fire at Merrilee.
"You reckon Lucas heard about this baby you
got yourself with and told his boy to stay away?
Then took his own advice and is staying away
from me too?"

"I don't know, Mama," Merrilee said,
misery welling up inside her. "I don't care about
the Procters."

Mama gripped her arm, hard. "Merrilee,
you ain't a little girl anymore that I can hold in
my lap and sing sweet little songs to. But now
you got yourself in this fix, and I suppose you
want me to help you out. Well, you know I
can't abide by no abortion, so I reckon you'll
have to have this kid. But you're going to have
to go to work, same as me, to contribute." She
released her arm with a shove. "So just forget
about school and go get yourself a job. We'd
better start saving our money for diapers and
such. Babies cost money."

"What about adoption, Mama?" Merrilee
said, her lip trembling.

Mama stared. "Girl, this is your cross to
shoulder. Not some puppy you go palming off on

others. Leastwise, that's what my mama told me when I got pregnant with you." She pushed the cigarette stub in the disposal and ground the blades. *"The pity of it is that you're making me shoulder this cross too."*

"Your mother wanted to keep the baby?" Nora said. "For you and her to raise together?"

Merrilee rose, turning to face the house, away from Nora's probing eyes. "She was willing." She cleared her throat. "You and Steven—you're church-goers, right?"

"Yes. We're members of a large Episcopalian church."

Merrilee didn't know anything about Episcopalians, outside of some folks at Gospel Fellowship referring to them as "stiff-necked tradition lovers." "But you pray and . . . and believe in Jesus?"

"Yes." Nora smiled. "How about you?"

"Oh yes, ma'am. I believe in him. That's why it's important that my baby be raised by Christians."

"Nora! Nora!" Steven rushed down the steps, followed by Lucky, who barked cheerfully, running ahead of his master.

Merrilee panicked and scrambled behind the swing, squatting to protect herself.

✳ ✳ ✳

"Steven! Merrilee, it's all right. I'll take Lucky up to the—"

"Merrilee?" Steven ran the last of the distance and gripped Lucky by the collar to hold the dog back. His face was puzzled. "What are you doing here?"

Merrilee stood up. "Nora invited me." She edged around the swing, using it now for protection, not from Lucky but from being seen by Steven. She felt uneasy in her swimsuit, stomach sticking out to there, her legs and arms all exposed.

Nora seemed to sense her discomfort and handed her a towel from the shed. "We've had a lovely time today, Steven. I was going to ask Merrilee to stay for dinner, if she'd like, so that we can discuss the baby."

Steven raised an eyebrow at his wife, and Merrilee instinctively realized all wasn't well between the couple. She knotted the towel around herself and headed toward the stairway. "I probably better be getting back. We can talk another—"

"No, stay, Merrilee," Steven said. He shot Nora a questioning look, who returned it with a gentle smile. His face relaxed, and he smiled, then turned to Merrilee, the tension gone. "As long as you're here, this would be a good chance to talk."

Merrilee glanced between husband and wife and

decided all was safe. Whatever argument they'd been
nursing had passed between them and flitted away
like one of the hummingbirds at the feeder. She'd
never seen such a quick end to a disagreement
between Mama and any of her male friends. Not one.

She smiled inwardly and touched her belly as she
climbed up the stairs with Steven and Nora behind
her, each with an arm wrapped around the other,
Lucky in tow.

✳✳✳✳✳✳✳✳✳✳✳✳✳✳✳✳✳✳✳✳✳✳

After putting Lucky in the laundry room, Nora hastily thawed thick steaks. She watched from the window as Steven fired up the outdoor grill and heard
Merrilee laugh when he donned his customary white
chef's hat and apron. Nora smiled as she stood at the
sink and rinsed baking potatoes. After popping them
into the oven, she joined Steven and Merrilee outside.

Hearing her leave the house, Lucky whined
loudly from his holding area.

"Are you sure he's okay?" Merrilee said, a worried expression on her face. "I'm sorry he needs to be
penned up."

"It's all right. He's fine." Nora said.

✳ ✳ ✳

She smiled at her husband. "I see Merrilee feels the same way about your barbecuing getup as I do."

"It's my good-luck outfit," Steven said to Merrilee. "If I don't wear it, the steaks burn."

"Merrilee, would you like to go have a long, warm bath while dinner cooks?" Nora said. "This'll take a while."

"That would feel good. I like swimming, but the chlorine always makes me itchy. Not that there's anything wrong with your pool," she added hastily.

Nora smiled and took her arm. "Come on. I'll show you to the guest bath."

When Merrilee was happily ensconced in the marble garden tub with the built-in whirlpool, Nora rejoined Steven outside. She put her hand on his arm. "Thank you for asking her to stay."

Steven set down the turning fork. "You've already decided how you want to handle this. All I can do is back you. She is a nice girl, and perhaps I should get a chance to know her better myself."

"But . . ."

He turned back to the steaks. "Let's see what she has to say tonight about her future with the baby, once we become the parents."

"Would it be so terrible if she wanted to stay involved?"

* * *

"No." He kissed the tip of her nose.

"It would give her some stability, Steven. A place to go, people who cared about her."

Steven studied her thoughtfully. "You do care about her, don't you? Pretty deeply too."

Nora nodded. "I want her to stay involved. I want to look out for her."

"Nora . . ."

"I have to believe God put this love for her in my heart because I prayed about being involved with her. I know she can still decide to keep the baby. But I don't believe she will. I don't believe they'll both leave our lives."

"We'll see. We have a few more weeks to find out."

****

"Dinner was wonderful, Nora. Great steaks, Mr. Rey." Merrilee smiled, then realized how much the effort hurt. A dull throb built at the back of her neck and spread upward.

"Call me Steven." He smiled at Merrilee over the empty dessert plates that Nora cleared from the table. "Did you get enough to eat?"

Merrilee patted her belly. She felt like she was

carrying twins. "More'n enough. I don't think this baby and I need to eat for about two weeks."

Steven cleared his throat. "Maybe this would be a good time to talk about him—"

"Her. It's a girl, Mr., er, Steven. I'm sure of it."

"I think she's right," Nora said, smiling at her husband as she rejoined them at the table. "Merrilee seems to be in good touch with this baby." She took Steven's hand and smiled broadly. "We'd better plan on a girl."

Steven looked uncomfortably at Nora, then Merrilee. "Anyway . . . I think it's time we talk about your plans for involvement after the baby's born."

"I think it's best I not be involved at all," she said. The dull throb was building into a dull roar in her brain, but she struggled to keep track of the conversation. "If I didn't think the baby'd be interested in her biological parents, I wouldn't even have my name on the birth certificate. But I don't want to make it difficult for her later, if she has questions or anything."

"We're willing for you to be involved in the baby's life," Nora said. "In fact, we'd welcome it."

Merrilee shook her head, swallowing the burning tears in her throat. Why did they have to talk about this? "No, ma'am. It wouldn't be right. I don't want her confused while she's growing up. She'll just

* * *

need one mommy . . . and a daddy. And you two
will be it."

"You have until the baby's born—even after—
to change your mind," Steven said.

"No, sir, I won't. This is what's best for everybody, especially her."

"But, Merrilee—"

She couldn't bear to see the stricken expression
on Nora's face. Couldn't she understand that what
she asked was too much for Merrilee to give? Wasn't
it enough that she was entrusting them with her
baby? Did they want her too?

Her head filled with a sound like a swarm of
bees, buzzing and stinging. Maybe this was what
Mama's sick headaches had felt like, what her whole
life had felt like.

Maybe the day she'd died, she just couldn't take
the noise anymore and chose the best solution she
could manage.

"Can I go sit on your sofa for a while?" Merrilee
said. "My head hurts something awful." Her vision
was getting dim from the headache, and the hum
inside her head intensified.

Steven guided her to the sofa, and she sat down.
Nora fussed over her, putting her feet up so that she
was lying down.

* * *

"Probably too much sun," she heard Steven say.

Someone draped a light blanket over her, then tucked her in. "Sleep well, Merrilee," Nora whispered softly, then kissed her forehead.

Merrilee sighed and curled into the blanket, instinctively curving one arm securely around her belly.

❊❊*❊*❊*❊*❊*❊*❊*❊*❊*❊*❊*❊*❊*

When Merrilee awoke, the room was pitch-black, save for the dim light of the moon shining through the windows. She sat up, grateful to find her headache diminished.

The kitchen microwave clock read four o'clock. Merrilee groaned, knowing Mrs. Pennywood would worry. Maybe even now the state troopers were out looking for her. Mrs. Pennywood had strict rules about curfew. Other girls had tested her on it, just for the sake of being contentious, but Mrs. Pennywood had a way of making them regret it by giving them extra homework after schooltime.

Merrilee heard a sharp whine from the laundry room, and she started. Then she remembered Lucky was inside, and she moved through the kitchen and cautiously approached the door. "Are you okay?" she whispered.

* * *

Lucky scratched the door and whined louder.

Merrilee bit her lip. What if he'd run out of food and water? What if he needed to go outside to go to the bathroom? She wouldn't care for being penned up if she were in similar straits.

"If I let you out, will you give me a head start so that I can run for the bathroom to close the door? Maybe you'll go find Nora and Steven, huh? I bet you know where their bedroom is. They'll let you outside."

Lucky whined once more, then abruptly stopped.

Merrilee's heart pounded. "Lucky?" She edged open the door, ready to make a run for it.

Lucky sat on his haunches, polite as a show dog. His tail swish-swished against the floor at the sight of her, but otherwise, he remained motionless.

"Well, I'll be." Merrilee pushed the door completely open.

Lucky remained in a sit-stay position. He whined, then panted.

"Good boy. That's a good boy," Merrilee crooned, slowly extending her hand. When he didn't move, she touched his head lightly, and when he still didn't move, she stroked him between the ears. "Why, you're just a big old pussycat!"

"Nora says that's what he thinks he is."

Merrilee turned. Steven stood at the other end of the kitchen, his hands jammed in the pockets of his bathrobe.

Lucky yelped and scurried toward him, winding himself around his legs.

"I hope Lucky and I didn't wake you up," she said.

"Not at all." Yawning, Steven moved to the counter and removed the carafe from the coffee-maker. "I always get up this early. Gives me a chance to think. Sometimes I go for a jog."

"I guess you'll be getting up this early a lot with the baby," Merrilee said, trying to joke. Without Lucky to pet anymore, she felt vulnerable.

"I'm sure I will." Steven smiled, coffee scoop poised over the filtered basket. "Do you want some of this?"

"No thanks."

"Oh, that's right. Sorry. It's not good for the baby."

"I never liked it much, anyway, though I used to drink it sometimes at night to keep myself awake until Mama got home from work."

"Where did she work?"

"At a little café in Palmwood. She was the lead

waitress for as long as I can remember, and whenever anybody was sick, she had to take their shift. Since the place was open from 6 A.M. to midnight, she could make good money."

"Who stayed with you when she was gone?" Steven flipped the coffeemaker's On switch.

"Nobody." Merrilee shrugged. "From about the time I was in first grade, I could take care of myself."

Steven studied her a moment, then opened the refrigerator door. "Would you like a glass of milk?"

"Sure." Merrilee took a seat at the table. Lucky sat beside her, then curled up at her feet. Merrilee smiled and reached down to pat him.

Steven brought her milk and his coffee to the table. "I hope you don't mind skim milk—that's all we have."

"I don't mind at all," she said, lying. To her way of thinking, it tasted more like water. She drank it anyway and at least found it good and cold.

"How's your headache?"

"Much better." She drained the glass and wiped her mouth with the back of her hand. Embarrassed that Steven had caught her in the action, she lowered both hands to her lap.

Steven smiled, as if he realized her embarrassment and wanted to put her at ease. "You and I

* * *

haven't had a chance to talk alone, and there's some-thing I've wanted to ask you."

"Wh-what?" She could think of a million ques-tions she didn't want to answer.

"I know you grew up without a father, so I imagine you're more than qualified to give me some ideas on what would make a good dad."

Merrilee silently let out a whoosh of relief. "That's easy enough."

"Really?" He raised an eyebrow.

"Sure. You love your kids no matter what they do or what happens to them."

"That's it?"

What kind of answer had he expected? "Yeah, that's it." She paused. "I've been reading the Bible since I was about eleven. And the more I read it, the more I see that message. If we belong to God—if we're his kids—he loves us no matter what." She was clinging to that belief now, even though lots of folks—and her own head, at times—had told her otherwise for months. But God knew the truth and loved her even more than she loved this baby.

"Do you believe that kind of love is possible for mortals?"

"What do *you* believe?" Merrilee drew a shallow breath and held it.

"I believe that it's only possible by faith . . . and God's grace."

Merrilee quietly exhaled. "I want my baby to be raised with that. I want her to have a Christian family."

"Nora and I are believers," Steven said.

Merrilee nodded. "That's what she said. I'm glad to hear you say it too. Only someone who understands God's love can give it in return. Just make sure that even if you're really angry at my baby about something she's done that you let her know you love her anyway. Sometimes—" She faltered, the memory of Mama intruding. Her voice dropped. "Sometimes you find out later you were wrong about everything."

Steven took her hand. "Would it surprise you if I said you seem to understand unconditional love better than anybody I know?"

She nodded.

"I don't know anybody else who has your unconditional love for a child. I'll do my best to always remember that love and sacrifice and match it with my own."

"You're going to be a great dad." She eased her hand from his. Such talk made her uncomfortable. "Nora said you two would come with me for my ultrasound in a few weeks. . . . Did she mention it?"

* * *

"Only about a hundred times last night. It's nice of you to ask us."

"I'll be happier with you there. I don't much like doctors' offices." Then, remembering he was a doctor himself, she hastily added, "You never know what's going to happen there."

Steven laughed. "I have many patients who think exactly the same way. Some of them are so nervous, they have to be pulled down from the waiting room walls. Me, I'm not keen on going to the dentist's office."

"Ha! That's nothing bad. All he does is check your teeth. Or maybe fill a cavity."

"The sound of the drill doesn't bother you?"

"Nope." Merrilee rose, yawning. "Maybe you'd better take me back to Adoption Lifeline. Mrs. Pennywood will be worried."

"We phoned her last night and let her know you were staying with us. Why don't you go back to sleep for a while? Nora can drive you home later in the morning."

She yawned again. "A little more sleep does sound good."

"Great." Steven smiled. "Thanks for chatting with me. I'm glad you spent some time with us."

"Me too. Good night. Again."

✳ ✳ ✳

She headed back to the couch, Lucky padding alongside her. Merrilee covered up, and Lucky plopped down on the floor beside her. "You're a good dog," Merrilee whispered, patting his head. She curled up under the blanket, secure and happy.

❋❋❋❋❋❋❋❋❋❋❋❋❋❋❋❋❋❋❋❋❋❋❋❋❋❋

Dear Baby Girl,

Now I know for sure you're going to have a great dad. Don't let a day go by without reminding yourself how fortunate you are to be with him.

Lucky's a nice dog too. You and he are going to be pals.

Five

The next two weeks reminded Merrilee later of the square of baking chocolate she'd bit into as a little girl: so appetizing to look at, so tasty at first bite, then acrid on the tongue. Time became bittersweet— an oxymoron, as her English teacher would have explained the literary term. When she wasn't attending Adoption Lifeline's school or doing chores around the maternity home, Merrilee spent most of her free time with the Reys.

* * *

Steven and Nora took her boating on the lake,
and she watched Nora ski. When Merrilee said that it
looked like fun and she'd love to try it—except for
the baby—she could see in Steven's eyes that he
wanted to say, *You can, after the baby's born.* Instead, he
turned away. He knew as well as she that their friendship would soon end. As much as she wanted to
become a part of their lives, she knew that she
couldn't.

Nora was the only one who acted as if nothing
would change. Against her better judgment, Merrilee
allowed herself to shop with Nora for baby things—
blankets, sheets, designer clothes as well as more practical sleepers and onesies. Nora even purchased a lacy
white outfit and said that she thought it would make
the perfect christening gown. Merrilee said she
thought it would too, then silently reminded herself
she wouldn't be around to see the baby wear it.

She wanted to stay away from the Reys. Each
time they called—or she found herself picking up the
phone because she was lonely and needed to chat—
she told herself it would be the last time. Then she
would have so much fun with them, feel so loved and
wanted, that she couldn't stop from thinking about
their next meeting.

While Merrilee admired the home, cars, and

* * *

boat, she realized that it wasn't their material possessions that brought out any envy in her. No, it was the
love Steven and Nora consistently regenerated
between themselves that spread outward to include
her.

She missed Mama's loving. As time grew closer
for her own baby's birth, she found herself wishing
she could crawl up in Mama's lap once again and be
comforted herself.

The day before the scheduled ultrasound, Mrs.
Pennywood called Merrilee into her office, then shut
the door for privacy. "Merrilee, I'm worried about
you," she said without fanfare.

"Why? The doctor said everything seems well.
And tomorrow we'll—"

Mrs. Pennywood shook her head. "Not the
baby. I'm worried about your emotional state. I
would never try to influence you one way or another
about signing the adoption release papers, but I'm
concerned that your continued involvement with the
Reys will make a final decision more difficult for
you."

Merrilee lifted her chin. "I told you, I told
them, that I'm signing those papers. I want them to
raise my baby. Why would spending time with them
change my mind?"

"Because the parting will be so much more difficult. Having a baby is emotional enough. After the
delivery, you may not be thinking clearly about
what's best for the baby. You may only be thinking
about how much greater your losses will be—not
only the baby but the Reys as well. And so you might
decide to keep the baby."

"I won't." Merrilee clenched her teeth. Why
wouldn't anybody believe her? How could she
explain that deep in her heart she knew this was what
God wanted, no matter how much it hurt? Surely he
would give her the strength, just as he had always for-
tified her in the past. Hadn't she always prayed that
he would?

Even her prayers for herself continually led back
to God's answer for her baby's future. No matter
how much she already ached with loneliness,
Merrilee couldn't raise her baby. Alone, she couldn't
give her daughter the kind of life she needed, something far removed from Palmwood.

That night Merrilee lay in bed, wishing she had
the strength to get up and write in the journal. She
hadn't written much in the past two weeks, since
she'd started spending so much time with the Reys.
A wave of guilt washed through her, as if she were
being disloyal. Every day she was squandering her

last few chances to talk to the baby. In scarcely a month, she'd be out of opportunities.

"I'll be back in Palmwood, and you'll still be here in Austin," she whispered, laying her hands on her belly. She would miss the giant curve of her stomach, would miss the physical touch. At times she almost felt as though her Baby Girl was pressing her tiny hands against Merrilee's—their own private, silent communication.

Tonight, however, the baby was quiet and still.

"I'll see you tomorrow," Merrilee whispered. "Really see you—well, at least an image of you—on the sonogram machine. Then in about a month, we can meet face-to-face, okay, Baby Girl?"

Merrilee pressed her hands against her belly.

The baby didn't respond.

"All right, then," Merrilee said, disappointed. She yawned and rolled uncomfortably to her side. "Sleep tight."

❋❋❋❋❋❋❋❋❋❋❋❋❋❋❋❋❋❋❋❋❋❋❋❋

"Steven, please hurry!" Nora called while she fussed with an earring. "We don't want to be late."

"We've got plenty of time," he said, but even he looked nervous as he straightened his tie with one hand and grabbed his car keys with the other.

❋ ❋ ❋

The drive into town seemed interminable. Nora chewed her lipstick off twice, a nervous habit she'd thought long kicked. *Hurry, hurry,* she sang inwardly. *We're going to see the baby today! Oh, hurry, hurry.*

"What if it's a boy?" Steven said. "Do you think Merrilee will be disappointed?"

"Probably. She's completely convinced this is a girl." Nora sighed happily. "I can't believe we're going to find out today. We're going to see our baby, Steven! Can you believe it?"

Steven considered for a moment. "We need to be careful of Merrilee's feelings during the ultrasound today."

"I know." Nora sobered. She wouldn't hurt Merrilee's feelings for anything in the world.

"More than that, we need to remember that Merrilee's a tangle of emotions, anyway. Being on the verge of saying good-bye to her child makes her doubly vulnerable to sadness. And Mrs. Pennywood says we can expect more signs of grief in these last few weeks before delivery. She said Merrilee might even refuse to see us."

"She wouldn't do that . . . would she?"

Steven shrugged. "Unless I miss my guess, what Mrs. Pennywood's trying to say in her delicate fashion is that maternal love is waging serious war with

Merrilee right now. And we may come out on the
losing side."

"With no baby?"

"That's one scenario. Another is an abrupt
closure to our friendship with Merrilee. You can't
expect her to simply say it's been fun, thanks for the
good times, then blithely walk away."

Nora felt torn. She understood what Steven was
saying, but she didn't know how to think beyond the
inevitable farewell, didn't know how to make things
better for any of them.

She would miss Merrilee too. More, she was
certain, than she even realized in this moment of joy.

****

"Scoot up on this table, Merrilee. That's a good girl."

The nurse lay a scratchy white sheet across
Merrilee's stomach, giving it an affectionate pat that
made Merrilee feel like Winnie the Pooh. "You doin'
all right, sugar?" the nurse asked.

Dressed in a paper gown, Merrilee suppressed
a shiver from a combination of fear and the air-
conditioning vent above the table. "I'm fine," she lied.

The nurse evidently believed her because she left
the room, leaving Merrilee alone.

* * *

Where are Nora and Steven?

She turned her head toward the bank of high-tech machinery beside the examining table and held her breath. The door opened behind her. Then Nora was at her side. Merrilee extended her hand closest to the machinery, and Nora took it between her own. Merrilee could feel that her own hand was cold and clammy in Nora's warm, confident one.

"I'm scared," she whispered.

"It won't hurt," Nora said. "They're just going to run a little microphone-looking thing over your tummy."

"I'm still scared." Merrilee gripped her hand tighter. "Where's Steven?"

"He's parking the car in the garage. I wish you'd let us pick you up."

"Mrs. Pennywood was going to visit a friend in the hospital, and since the doctor's office is just next door—"

The door swung open, and a woman in pastel scrubs entered, a chart in her hand, all smiles. "Hi, Merrilee. I'm Barbara, and I'll be helping you take a look at your baby today."

"Hi," Merrilee said, trying to sound brave, but her voice came out small and funny.

Barbara took a seat at the machinery and busied

herself with preparations. "I'm glad to see you brought your mom along, Merrilee."

Nora frowned. "I'm not her mother. I'm—"

"She's my friend," Merrilee cut in. "Her name is Nora. Nora Rey. And her husband, Steven, will be here in a moment. I asked them to be here."

Barbara glanced at the chart, then took a longer look. "Oh." She read a bit more and smiled again at Merrilee. This time her expression was more compassionate than chipper. "I understand, honey. Mrs. Rey, if you'll stand on the other side of the table we'll get started."

Nora complied, while Barbara turned the monitor toward them and punched a few buttons and dials. Merrilee drew a deep breath and smiled at Nora, then turned her attention to the monitor. Nora took her hand again and smoothed back Merrilee's hair. The action made Merrilee feel younger than her fifteen years, yet comforted.

"This is warm gel, Merrilee," Barbara said, holding up a squeeze bottle. "I have to put it on your abdomen so that the transducer can make good contact, all right?"

Merrilee nodded, biting her lip.

Barbara lifted the paper gown and lowered the sheet just enough to expose Merrilee's rounded belly.

* * *

She squirted gel, and Merrilee flinched, laughing. "That *is* warm."

Barbara smiled. "Can you see the monitor? How about you, Mrs. Rey?"

"Yes, just fine. Where is Steven?" she murmured. "He's going to miss everything!"

Barbara touched the tip of the transducer to Merrilee and rolled it around until a shadowy image appeared. "There're your baby's feet, Merrilee," she said. "See that there? She's a smart girl—head down, just like she's supposed to be. And there's her little rump. . . ."

"What are all those white lines?" Nora said, her voice catching in her throat.

"Those are bones. There's a leg . . . here's her pelvis. . . ."

Merrilee forgot her fear, fascinated with the pictures of her baby. "It's really a girl?" she whispered.

Barbara grinned. "She sure is. See right here? That's where we look. And farther up here are her ribs and—" Barbara broke off, her brow furrowing as she waved the transducer across Merrilee's skin.

"I thought maybe you could tell it was a girl by an extra rib," Nora said, laughing, then smiled down at Merrilee. "Remember the story of God taking a rib from Adam so that he could make woman?"

"We don't have to worry about names for boys anymore," Merrilee said, smiling back at Nora. "Now all we have to do is come up with a girl's name."

Barbara abruptly swiveled the monitor away from their view, still working the transducer.

Merrilee gripped Nora's hand, instinct taking over.

"Is something wrong?" Nora asked Barbara.

Barbara glanced up, her eyes sorrowful. "Dr. Welch will want to have a look, ladies. Excuse me." She all but sprinted for the door, passing Steven without speaking.

He turned to them for explanation. "Did she forget something?"

Nora squeezed Merrilee's hand but didn't let go. "We saw the baby, and then she turned the monitor away. Like she didn't want us to see. She's gone to get the doctor."

"I'm sure he wants to have a look for himself," Steven said, moving to Merrilee's side. "How ya doing, kiddo?"

"I . . . I'm not sure." She was too scared to talk, and besides, Mama would probably say that talking could jinx things.

The door opened, and Steven moved beside

Nora while the doctor entered. He nodded curtly at them, then, without speaking, held a stethoscope to Merrilee's abdomen. After listening intently, he moved the stethoscope several times. He nodded at Barbara, who handed him the transducer. Like her, he rolled it over the goo on Merrilee's stomach and studied the monitor.

At last he exchanged a glance with Barbara and nodded once. He laid down the transducer, and Barbara quietly left the room, her head bowed.

Merrilee clenched Nora's hand, feeling faint. She felt Steven's hand rest against her shoulder, and she lay still and quiet.

"There's no easy way to say this," the doctor said, looking first at Merrilee, then the Reys, then back to Merrilee. "But the baby's dead."

"No!" Nora's voice was vehement, accusing.

"Are you certain?" Steven asked quietly. "Aren't there more tests you can run?"

"Merrilee, has the baby been still lately?" Dr. Welch said. "When's the last time you remember him moving?"

"It's a girl, Doctor," Merrilee said softly. "And it was sometime yesterday, I think."

"No movement this morning?"

Merrilee shook her head. "I can't remember

any. I thought she was just sleeping. I didn't know something was wrong."

"Of course you didn't." He rested a hand on her head, smiling sadly.

"But what happened?" Nora said.

"I'm not sure, Mrs. Rey. The ultrasound doesn't reveal any abnormality with the baby or the placenta. It's possible we may never know." He paused. "My main concern right now is that the baby be delivered. Whatever the cause of death, we don't want to put Merrilee in jeopardy too."

Fear entangled with the sorrow already gripping Merrilee's insides. "Delivered? But . . . but . . ."

The doctor leaned down close, so he could speak directly to Merrilee. "We can sedate you and do a C-section. . . . Do you know what that is?"

"Where you cut me open and take the baby out?"

He nodded. "Or we could give you drugs to induce labor. You'd be awake for that."

Nora turned her head away, shutting her eyes.

"I want to be awake," Merrilee said, her voice calm. "I want to see my baby being born." She turned toward Nora and Steven. "And I'd like you two with me . . . if you want to be."

"Of course we do, Merrilee," Steven said. He bent and kissed her cheek.

* * *

Nora opened her eyes. Seeing her grief-stricken expression, Merrilee felt as if her own heart would break. She had had such dreams. They all had.

"I'm so sorry, Nora," she whispered, her eyes wet. "I'm so . . ." Sobbing, she laid her hands on her belly. "Oh, Baby Girl!"

Through her grief, she vaguely felt Nora press a hand over her own and Steven touching her shoulder.

"We'll be there," Nora said. "Whatever you want . . . we'll be there for you."

✳✳✳✳✳✳✳✳✳✳✳✳✳✳✳✳✳✳✳✳✳✳✳✳

Suddenly everyone was all action. Mrs. Pennywood was located, and acting as Merrilee's guardian, she signed the necessary papers. An orderly and a nurse came down from an upper floor of the hospital to take Merrilee away in a wheelchair. A stout, fiftyish nurse promised that Nora and Steven could join her later.

"I want Nora to go with me," Merrilee said, clamping her hand around the wheelchair's brake lever.

"But, dear, she's not family. She's not even a legal guardian."

✳ ✳ ✳

"I want her to go with me," Merrilee insisted in a low voice.

"Please?" Nora said. "I'm the adoptive mother of the baby. . . . I'm also Merrilee's friend."

The nurse wavered. "All right. But only you. Your husband will have to wait until it's time for her to deliver. I'll take Merrilee up to the sixth floor. You can join us there." She signaled to the orderly, who hustled Merrilee into the elevator without giving her a chance to speak.

Steven kissed Nora on the cheek and drew her into his embrace. "Can I bring you anything? Something to read?"

She shut her eyes, wishing she could shut out the past hour as well. "Nothing, Steven." Her eyes watered. "I can't believe this is happening to her. She doesn't deserve this."

Steven held her closer. "Father," he whispered, "we don't understand why this is happening. We're grieving for the baby, but we're also grieving for Merrilee. She's just a girl, too young to go through this at all, much less with no parents to be with her. Help us to fill those shoes and give us the strength and wisdom to walk through the valley of the shadow of death alongside her."

Steven gently released Nora. "I'll make a few

phone calls. Then I'll hang around the sixth-floor
waiting room. They'll get me when it's time for
Merrilee to go to the delivery room."

"It could take hours, Steven. Just because . . .
just because the baby's dead, it doesn't mean that this
will go any faster."

"I'll call the office to have Mary reschedule all
my appointments for the next few days. This is where
I need to be."

"I love you." Her eyes filled with tears. "I love
you so much."

"I love you too, Blondie," he whispered. "Give
Merrilee my love. I'll be praying for you both."

Nora turned away, then back again. The walk
to the elevator seemed impossibly long. "How am
I going to help her?"

Steven held her close again. "You're just going
to have to walk into the fiery furnace and trust that
God is with you, Nora. That's all you can do. Now
go to her. She needs you, and you need her. You're
going to help each other."

****

The nurse, who said her name was Ingrid, had
Merrilee hooked up to an IV in record time, even

before she could panic at the sight of the needle. Merrilee was grateful to see Nora arrive.

"We were just getting started," Ingrid said, after introducing herself to Nora. "If either of you has any questions—any concerns at all—don't hesitate to speak up. I just started my shift, so I'll be on duty for twelve hours. I'll be your nurse exclusively, Merrilee, and I'll be with you from here until delivery, then afterward, okay?"

Merrilee nodded, pressing her lips together to keep from crying. If she started bawling, it would only make Nora feel bad.

Nora slipped her hand into hers, and Merrilee relaxed.

"I'm going to give you the drug—it's called Pitocin—that will bring on your labor. I'll be checking on you occasionally to see how the labor's progressing."

She paused, her expression sorrowful. "Honey, this is a bum deal, and I know you're hurting emotionally. I'm proud of you for wanting to see your baby born—I don't think you'll regret it later. I've never had a patient tell me she did."

"You've been through this before? With other women?" Merrilee said.

Ingrid nodded, fussing with the IV line. "Did you take a Lamaze class?"

Merrilee's eyes watered. Thankfully, Nora answered for her. "We didn't get a chance."

"When we get to the hard part of labor, I'll be showing you how to breathe to help with the pain. And to calm yourself. Mrs. Rey, you can do them with Merrilee." Ingrid stepped away from the IV stand. "There. The Pitocin's started. I'll monitor the level to make sure your contractions aren't so far apart that nothing happens, or so close together that you can't catch your breath. If the pain does get too bad, we can give you a pill to relax you, or even a shot that will numb you from the waist down."

"I don't like shots," Merrilee mumbled.

Ingrid smiled in sympathy. "Just keep it in mind in case you want some relief. But don't wait too long because if you get the urge to push, it's too late then. Let me go check on a few things, ladies, and then I'll be back."

When she'd gone, Nora pulled up a chair beside the bed.

Merrilee stared at the IV, unable to look at her.
Drip, drip, drip.

Merrilee shut her eyes.

"Merrilee, I'm so sorry," Nora whispered. "This is such a shock. I don't know what else to say. What can I do for you?"

* * *

"Nothing."

Drip, drip.

They sat together, silent, for several hours. Merrilee kept her eyes squeezed shut.

The rippling began in her belly, pains so light at first that she scarcely noticed them.

At last Nora cleared her throat. "Can I call someone for you? Your friend Sylvie, maybe?"

"There's no one to call." Merrilee kept her eyes shut, but she imagined she could hear the liquid pouring into her veins, forcing her body to expel the baby.

She needed Mama to hold her and sing, to see her through this. But Mama was gone.

How they'd laugh back in Palmwood when she returned with an empty belly and the knowledge that her Baby Girl was dead.

"Nora?"

"Yes? I'm here."

"I didn't ever tell you about Mama's death."

"No, you didn't."

"Or about Wayne."

"No, you didn't tell me much about him either."

"Mama was disappointed when she found out I was pregnant. She'd always told me to stay away from boys, get myself a good education, and become somebody. But when she knew about the baby, she told me to forget all that. That I was going to have to work, same as her, to support the baby."

"What about Wayne?" Nora said softly. "He could have at least contributed financially. It was his responsibility as the father."

Merrilee felt a tear trickle from her eyes. The pains were increasing. "I didn't want anything to do with him. His daddy had been hanging out with Mama for a while, and one day when ol' Lucas came to visit, he brought his son, Wayne. Lucas wanted to be alone with Mama, so he gave Wayne some money and told him to treat me right. Just like that, he said, 'Treat her right, boy,' and laughed. Like they had some kind of joke between them."

"Then what happened?" Nora asked gently.

"It was the tail end of summer, still hot, so I put my bathing suit on under my clothes, and we headed for a stock pond off a country road. On the way there, Wayne stopped and bought some beer. I'd never had it before, but he said, go on, don't be a baby, and didn't my mama drink it?

"Anyway, I was feeling kind of good about having a fella notice me, even if his daddy did pay for him to do so. I popped a top and took a sip. He laughed and said, no, Merrilee, ya got to swallow it

down real quick. By the time we got to the pond, I'd
drunk two."

She heard Nora shift in the chair beside the
bed. "You don't have to talk about this if you don't
want to."

Merrilee bit back a groan.

Nora rose. "Are you having a contraction?"

She nodded, unable to speak for a moment. The
pain was dull but fast, like someone closing a fist
around her insides. When it subsided, she felt her
breathing slow to normal and found the nurse beside
her.

"The Pitocin's working," Ingrid said. "Let's
have a look and see how far you've dilated."

She pulled back the sheet and examined
Merrilee, who stared up at the acoustic tiles in the
ceiling. Nora sat beside her, lending silent support.

"You're already to four centimeters, almost to
five," Ingrid said, lowering the sheet. "The contractions will start coming harder now. When they do,
try breathing like this. Mrs. Rey, you watch too. It'll
be easy for Merrilee to lose her focus, and you may
need to get right down in her face and remind her."

They watched while Ingrid demonstrated. Then
they each practiced panting and hee-hee-hee-hoo-ing
in rhythm. Ingrid smiled, then left them alone—

* * *

"Just for a bit because I think things are going to speed up soon."

When they were alone again, Merrilee leaned back and tried to collect her thoughts. She wanted to be ready when the pain came again. She also wanted to finish telling Nora the whole story. "You can probably figure out what happened."

"After that boy got you drunk?" Nora said.

Merrilee nodded. "At first it was fun. We were just goofing around, I thought, being silly. Then when I realized Wayne didn't have any intention of stopping, I got scared. He was acting mean, calling me a tease, saying I didn't have to act so innocent-like. Everybody knew what my mama was like and that I wasn't any different."

"But you were, Merrilee," Nora said softly. "And you still are."

The pain began again, low in Merrilee's insides. "It didn't matter. Even after he realized he'd been wrong, he looked real sorry but said no one would believe I'd told him no. If I wouldn't say anything, he wouldn't either.

"By the time he dropped me home, I was so sick, I went straight to bed. When I woke up the next morning, Lucas was still there. He winked and asked me if I'd had a good time with his son, and I

knew then that he thought the same as Wayne had.
That everybody did."

The pain rose. She let out a moan, the contraction cresting.

Nora got to her feet. "Breathe, Merrilee.
Breathe."

Merrilee did, and when she'd made it through
and lay back down, she was surprised to find she was
crying.

Nora stroked the wet hair back from her face.
"What about your mother? Surely she believed you."

She shook her head. "Mama was hungover all
day and didn't get up until supper time. Then she had
to get ready for her shift, and I tried to tell her, but
she waved me off with one of her sick headaches.
I waited up to talk when she came home, knowing
she'd have drunk a bunch of coffee and be feeling
better. But the first thing she said was, 'Well,
Merrilee, I saw Wayne and he said you two didn't hit
it off yesterday. It's probably just as well, what with
me seeing his daddy and all.'"

"But you told her the truth?"

Merrilee shook her head. "I figured it was over,
and there was no point in being a crybaby about it."

"But you got pregnant. Surely then you told
your mother."

"Not right away. Mama had a big falling out with Lucas Procter. He'd taken up with some woman he'd met in a bar, and Mama regularly threatened to go shoot her, him, or both of them. Wayne had left town by then, and if Mama knew what he'd done to me, she might have gotten liquored up and shot his daddy instead."

Merrilee felt the next wave coming, and she braced herself. "Besides, she right away assumed I'd been agreeable with Wayne. And there she'd been trying to teach me to stay away from boys, study hard, and all that."

"Oh, Merrilee. She would have understood."

"No, ma'am. Mama was getting sadder and sadder every day. The men weren't coming around anymore, and she started drinking heavier. Me being pregnant changed her whole attitude toward me. She stopped loving me, it seemed like, stopped singing songs to me at night like she used to, even when I was too old for such things. She started yelling at me, something she never used to do.

"Finally, one night, she yelled at me about something I'd done wrong, and she called me a tramp. I couldn't take it anymore, and I told her if I was a tramp, then she was the one who taught me, and did she even care that while she was boozing it up with Lucas Procter, his son was forcing himself on me?

"She got real quiet, and then she started crying. I felt bad for having talked to her that way—she was out of her head drunk and didn't know what she'd been saying. I tried to tell her I was sorry. She just held me close, pulled me into her lap, even, and rocked me for a long time. 'My little girl,' she said over and over.

"When she finally stopped crying, I thought everything would be okay then. She gave me some money and asked me to go up to the trailer park office and buy her some cigarettes. That she'd cook us some supper when I returned."

Merrilee's voice broke against the knifing pain. "I heard the shot when I was coming back. We all went running, but it was too late."

A sob tore from her throat, lifted to the tiled ceiling, and fell into pieces around her. The pain took her away on sharp wings.

Nora stroked her hair, her wet cheeks, her hands, bending low to whisper. "I'm sorry, Merrilee. I'm so sorry. It's all right. I'm here."

Merrilee groped for Nora's arm. She wanted to ask her not to leave, that she couldn't bear it again.

"I'm here, Merrilee," she heard Nora say, as if

from a distance. Then her face was right next to hers. "Breathe, sweetie. Like this—remember? Hee-hee-hee . . ."

The pain rocketed inside her, and she tried to comply.

"You're a brave, strong girl, Merrilee," Nora said. "You're doing fine. You always have. You've done right by this baby. Jesus knows you have."

An image of the crucifixion flashed through Merrilee's mind, a horrible scene with darkness and lightning like something out of a horror movie. Then Mama's words returned, swift and sharp: *"The pity of it is that you're making me shoulder this cross too."*

She'd shouldered it just long enough to accompany Merrilee to Calvary. Then she'd left her only child alone.

My God, my God, why have you forsaken me?

"Mama!" she cried out, and the pain subsided, then returned double force.

****

"Her labor moved so quickly, they didn't have time to give her anything for the pain," Nora said hurriedly to Steven, as they donned paper surgical clothes. "Even the nurse was surprised. She's prepping Merrilee now, and we're supposed to meet them in the delivery room."

"Is Merrilee all right—emotionally, I mean?"

Nora shook her head, and a tear splashed onto the paper mask.

"How about you, Nora?"

The door swung open. "Dr. and Mrs. Rey? You'd better hurry. The baby's crowning."

They followed the unfamiliar nurse to the delivery room. The entire room looked green, from the tiles to the scrubs on Dr. Welch at the foot of the table and the nurses encouraging Merrilee. A plastic bassinet sat nearby.

Farther away stood an unplugged warming table.

"Thank goodness you're here." Ingrid ushered them to Merrilee's side, where the girl reclined against a backrest. "She's been asking for you."

"I thought you wouldn't make it," Merrilee said, looking better now that she could fight the pain by pushing when the doctor commanded. She strained forward, her face contorting with the effort. "She's . . . almost . . . here."

"That's it, Merrilee," Dr. Welch said. "Push! Here're the shoulders. . . . Once more!"

Nora put her arms under Merrilee. "Come on, sweetie, push," she said. "You can do it."

* * *

"And here she is," Dr. Welch said, handing off Merrilee's baby to a waiting nurse with a towel while he finished up.

The room grew quiet. Too quiet. Nora was conscious of the absence of the usual bustle and cries associated with a baby's birth, and she blinked back tears.

Merrilee leaned back against the backrest to catch her breath, and Nora wiped her brow. "Can you see her?" Merrilee whispered. "Is she pretty?"

"They'll bring her to you, Merrilee," Ingrid said, her voice somber. "Let them take a few measurements and clean her up a bit. Then you can hold her."

As she spoke, the nurse with the baby brought her to Merrilee and solemnly handed her over. Nora stood alongside and watched as Merrilee drew back the blanket to greet her perfectly formed, perfectly still baby girl.

Merrilee wept silently and held her close, while Nora turned into Steven's arms and released her own quiet tears.

****

They brought the baby again to Merrilee's room, and she and Nora bathed her side by side, then dressed her in the white christening gown. They shared sad smiles when it dwarfed her small body.

"You haven't held her yet," Merrilee said, cradling the baby, touching her cheek with awe.

"It doesn't seem right somehow," Nora said, a lump in her throat. "I don't want to intrude."

Merrilee turned. "She's your baby too." She handed her to Nora.

In her arms, the baby felt light, hardly more than a small pillow. Nora stared at the tiny, sweet face, and she swallowed hard. "You gave this baby everything, Merrilee. You gave her a chance she wouldn't have had with a girl who'd chosen abortion."

"I guess it didn't matter much, though, did it?" Merrilee said bitterly. "Maybe it would have been better for all of us if that's what I'd chosen way back there."

"You chose a harder road."

"One that cost Mama her life."

"That was your mother's choice. Not yours," Nora said quietly. "What matters is that even though this baby's conception and life inside your womb caused great pain, you loved her without reservation."

Nora's eyes welled with tears, and she handed the baby back. "And grace is never cheap. Or easy. Ask God."

❋❋❋❋❋❋❋❋❋❋❋❋❋❋❋❋❋❋❋❋❋❋❋❋❋

Merrilee did. During the next day that they kept her in the hospital, while the hospital photographer took a photo and snipped a lock of her daughter's hair as a keepsake, while the doctor sadly said they couldn't determine the cause of death, while she held her baby one last time and wept when she handed her over to be cremated, she asked God.

What had she done wrong? Hadn't she turned the other cheek when others cast stones? Hadn't she always chosen the baby ahead of herself? Hadn't she always taken care of Mama . . . ?

Oh, Mama. Now I have two gaping places in my heart that can never be filled.

Steven and Nora brought her flowers, a small vase with pale, full roses. She wanted to thank them, but she could barely speak, could barely endure their presence. They were grieving too, she knew, but the sorrow on their faces only intensified the guilt in her heart. She'd let them down.

When the doctor said she was well enough to go home, Merrilee filled a plastic hospital sack with her meager belongings. Mrs. Pennywood would pick her up, then take her back to Adoption Lifeline.

* * *

"You can stay for a few days, if you need to think about things," she'd said.

But Merrilee knew she couldn't spend one night in a home filled with pregnant girls such as she'd been. Her stomach felt empty and gnawing.

"Merrilee?" Nora knocked on the half-open door, then entered. Steven followed closely behind, carrying a large bag. "You're packing?" Nora said.

"They're booting me out," Merrilee said, trying to smile. "Mrs. Pennywood should be here soon." She tossed a comb, the final item, into the bag. "I'm catching a bus this afternoon for home."

"Palmwood?" Steven said.

She nodded, then sat on the edge of the bed, unable to meet their gaze.

Nora sat beside her and touched her shoulder. "We have another suggestion, one we hope you'll like." She glanced at Steven, smiling. "We want you to come live with us."

Merrilee raised her eyes. "What do you mean, live with you?"

"We're interested in becoming your legal guardians," Steven said. "Perhaps, in time—if you're willing—to even adopt you."

Merrilee's heart lifted, then fell. "That's a crazy idea."

"Is it?" Nora said. "We've gotten to know each other in a short period of time. Not to mention that we've shared the loss of your child."

"You should be trying to adopt another baby," Merrilee mumbled.

"We can't," Nora said simply.

"That's right. You're getting too old."

"We want you, Merrilee," Steven said quietly.

Merrilee's eyes filled with tears. They had worked their way into her heart and even now wouldn't leave. "I don't want to be the booby prize you win because you didn't get your first choice."

"Is that what you think?" Nora smiled sadly. "I was wondering how I was going to let you go after the baby was born! And now . . ." She shook her head. "Now we have even more in common, more that's entwined our lives. For years I thought God intended me to receive—a baby. And you've thought he was asking you to give up yours. But he's calling me to give to you, Merrilee, and for you to receive. From me. It's his blessing for each of us—to be together."

"I shouldn't have told you about Wayne—and Mama," Merrilee said.

"Why? Because you think I pity you now?"

"Well . . ."

"I'm sorry those things happened to you, but I admire you more than I pity you. Pity is for people who can't help themselves. You're the strongest person I know. I'd like you as my daughter because I could learn from you. As well as, hopefully, teach you in return."

"It wouldn't work, Nora," Merrilee said. "I'm sorry. Our connection was the baby, and now she's gone."

"Did you name her, Merrilee?" Steven said.

"Yeah, when they brought around the papers for me to sign, I listed her name as Grace. I thought about what y'all said about me loving her and sacrificing for her. I hope, at least, she knew she had all that going for her."

"I'm sure she did." Steven smiled.

"Well." Merrilee rose and picked up the bag. She had to get out of here—fast. Her hand rested briefly on the smaller stomach under her maternity blouse. "Like I said, Mrs. Pennywood will be here soon. I think the nurse said I have to leave in a wheelchair, even though I feel perfectly capable of walking."

"There's nothing we can say to change your mind?" Steven said.

"Nothing to convince you that we only want

to share a bit of the same grace with you that you shared with your daughter?" Nora added.

Merrilee shook her head, blinking back tears.

Nora hugged her, trying hard to smile. "I love you, Merrilee," she whispered. "You will always be the child of my heart. Know that I'm praying for you daily."

Merrilee nodded silently.

Nora stepped away, wiping her eyes.

Steven withdrew two packages—one small, one large. "We wanted you to have these," he said. "The large one has been for you—Nora's planned to give it to you for a while but hasn't had a chance. The other was for the baby. We thought you should have it."

He kissed her on the cheek, and she saw her own sorrow reflected in his eyes. "Good-bye, Merrilee. If you ever need anything, you know where we are."

Steven took his wife's arm, and they left the room.

Merrilee sat on the bed, her vision blurred. She opened the first package to find a Nancy Drew mystery, the next one she needed in the series.

With trembling fingers, she opened the next package to find a white shiny box.

✳ ✳ ✳

Inside was a small sterling silver–filigreed jewelry box in the shape of a heart. When she lifted the lid, a lullaby wafted out.

Jesus loves me, this I know . . .

Merrilee shut the lid and gripped the box tightly.

Six

Nora listlessly spooned dog food into Lucky's dish. He wagged his tail, nearly upsetting his water dish. "We haven't been around much lately, have we, boy?" she said, scratching him behind his ears. "We'll get back into the swing of things, I guess."

She rinsed the can before tossing it in the recycling bin, then stared at the papasan chair. She should have given it to Merrilee.

Steven put his arm around her.

* * *

"I suppose you're going to say I told you so," Nora said bitterly. "My heart's been broken twice in the past few days."

He kissed her temple, saying nothing.

Nora turned into his arms and rested her cheek against his chest. No matter how great her grief, she would never forget that Merrilee's was greater.

Jesus, comfort Merrilee now. Remind her that you love her.

Lucky looked up from his food and barked. A car door slammed, and the dog raced for the front door. Whining, he scratched the paint with his claws.

Steven glanced out the front window, then smiled at Nora. He nodded, as if in answer to her unspoken question.

Nora went to the door, her pulse racing. In her haste to get outside, she neglected to hold Lucky back. The dog shot out the door and jumped on Merrilee, who was trying to pay the cabbie. Sizing up the German shepherd, the cab driver jumped into his car, tossed Merrilee's suitcase and the paper bag out the window, and sped away.

Merrilee turned and faced Nora and Steven. When they didn't speak, she looked down at the ground.

Nora moved forward and embraced her, her eyes filling with tears.

✳ ✳ ✳

After a moment, Merrilee pulled back. "Is the invitation still good?" she whispered.

Nora cupped Merrilee's chin and gently raised her face. The scar on the bridge of her nose glistened, and Nora brushed back her hair. She was beautiful, so beautiful, the child of her dreams all these years. "Of course," she said, then couldn't speak for the emotion tightening her throat.

Merrilee glanced at Steven. "If it's okay . . . ?" she said hesitantly.

He nodded, then wrapped his arms around them both, his throat working up and down.

Lucky barked, started to jump into the group, then instead sat back on his haunches, whining. He followed them as they gathered Merrilee's bags and together headed inside the house.

****

Dear Baby Girl,

This is the last time I'm going to write. So much has happened, but then you know all that. Sometimes I think maybe you're watching from heaven, but other times I believe you're having too much fun with Jesus and everybody else to concern yourself with what's going on here.

* * *

But I do know that one day we'll meet face-to-face. You'll be much bigger, of course, but somehow I'll know you and you'll know me. I hope you're the one who takes my hand and introduces me to Jesus. I can't wait to meet both of you.

Meanwhile, Nora's calling, and I have to go. She's built a fire in the fireplace, and we're going to have a little ceremony of burning this journal. Today, you see, would have been your first birthday. She and I have talked and worked through a lot of things together. Steven too. We're all trying to look forward, not back, though of course I'll never forget you.

I haven't written in this journal since before you left this earth, but I wanted to give it back to you. Will you catch the ashes as they rise in the air? I hope they are a pleasing aroma to God as well, because he is the only one who could have shown me such Grace.

I love you always and hope you rest in Jesus' arms so that he can sing all the lullabies you want. I know he does for me.

Your mother,
Merrilee Hunter Rey

About the Author

A native Texan, Jane Orcutt lives in her home state with her husband and their two teenage sons. They have four four-legged pets—a German shepherd mix, a Pembroke Welsh corgi, and two lazy but mischievous cats.

Jane enjoys writing relationship-oriented books and loves happy endings. In addition to writing, her interests are trivia, history, current events, reading, and any games that involve letters and words. When she wants to be thoroughly humbled, she attempts to work the Sunday *New York Times* crossword puzzle. Jane is also an avid baseball fan, but she still has trouble understanding the infield-fly rule and how to calculate the Magic Number.

fiction.

Sierra's Story 0-8423-8726-9
Ryun's Story 1-4143-0003-4
Kenzie's Story 1-4143-0002-6

Kyra's Story 0-8423-8284-4
Miranda's Story 0-8423-8283-6
Tyrone's Story 0-8423-8285-2

THE LAMB AMONG THE STARS SERIES

The Shadow at Evening 1-4143-0067-0
The Power of the Night 1-4143-0068-9

Other thirsty(?) fiction

Love Rules 0-8423-8727-7
Dear Baby Girl 1-4143-0093-X

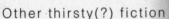

nonfiction.

Walk 0-8423-6069-7

Come Clean 0-8423-8358-1

Walking with Frodo 0-8423-8554-1

Walking with Bilbo 1-4143-0131-6

tap into life.

COMING SUMMER 2005 . . .

Dating
Mr. Darcy

*The smart girl's guide to
sensible romance*

THE NEW BOOK
BY SARAH ARTHUR

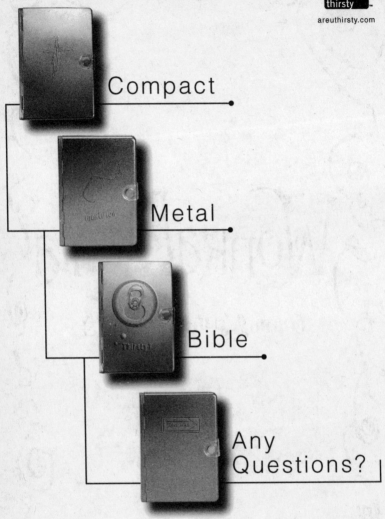

Compact

Metal

Bible

Any
Questions?

Available wherever Bibles are sold

areUthirsty.com

well . . . are you?

PREGNANT?

NEED HELP?

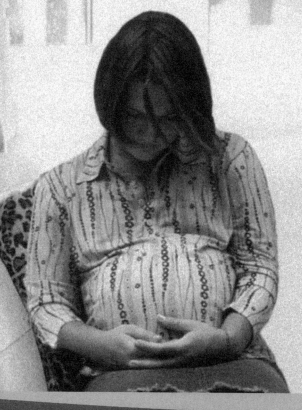

YOU HAVE OPTIONS:

CALL 800·395·HELP

OR GO TO WWW.PREGNANCYCENTERS.ORG